TO THE
GALLOWS

ELIZABETH SKARPNES

TO THE GALLOWS

ELIZABETH SKARPNES

This book is a work of fiction. The story, all names, characters, and incidents portrayed in this production are fictitious. No identification with actual persons (living or deceased), places, buildings, and products is intended or should be inferred.

First published in the United States of America in August 2024 by Second Cup Publishing, LLC.
www.elizabethskarpnes.com

ISBN 979-8-9893051-0-0 (paperback)
ISBN 979-8-9893051-1-7 (ebook)

Book cover design by Elizabeth Skarpnes

Content warnings are available on the author's website.

To my husband—I finally put it into words.
I love you this much.

Preface

While this book is generally light, fluffy, and all around cozy—please always check the content warnings for any book you read to make sure you are keeping yourself safe.

These can be found on my website at
www.elizabethskarpnes.com/gallows
or in the reading guide.

Pronunciation guide & reading guide
are available via QR code on the last page or at
www.elizabethskarpnes.com/ttg-home

Enjoy.

Chapter 1

Lorali

It was a shame that Eldric Lorecaster must die. Though he was a crook and a thief, his greatest crime was getting caught.

As a cleric of Ostara, Lorali could never voice approval for the way he and his compatriots took it upon themselves to redistribute the wealth within the city. But she couldn't help but wonder if this was justice or punishment—a part of her aching for the hungry mouths that looked to her, the tiniest hands praying for help outside the Order's doors day in and day out. His death would be a message to them all.

She waited, duty bound, at the foot of the wooden construct for the outlaw with prayer beads clutched tight in her fair, freckled palms. Though she could not change his fate, she could give his soul a last prayer before he was sent to Ostara's awaiting embrace. The square was quiet, only the echoing sound of his shackles reverberating off the dirt aisle and the sound of rustling wings as corvids perched along the rooftops. For all those he had ever helped, not one person cried out or moved to intervene. They watched with a mourner's stare, lamenting his death before it happened.

Her stomach twisted in knots, nausea washing over her as Eldric was marched down the aisle. She closed her eyes, taking measured breaths to calm her racing heart, reaching for the two rings laced on a necklace that lay just beneath her robes for comfort. This was not the first time she had met prisoners at the foot of the gallows to offer a last prayer, but as each step echoed across the quiet square, Lorali was filled with a sinking feeling she couldn't quite shake.

A throat cleared, and her eyes flew open to find the standard issue cotton shirt worn by all those she met here. It hung loose across his shoulders, a deep cut revealing the winter-paled skin of his chest. She had to tilt her head back to meet his clover-green eyes.

"Which god do you wish to invoke for your last rite, Sir Eldric?" Lorali's voice did not falter. It carried firm and sure, unwavering in the face of her duties to be performed. The corner of his lip quirked up into a wry smile.

"I am no sir, just Eldric will do."

"Eldric," Lorali amended. "Who do you wish to invoke for your last rite?"

"Dealer's choice," he said with an air of casual ease that earned a not so gentle shove from the unfamiliar guardsman. With his hands bound behind him, he could not catch himself and stumbled into her space. Lorali couldn't help the way her lips tilted downward as she reached out a hand to steady him. She was familiar with most of the guardsmen who brought prisoners to the gallows, but she didn't recognize this one's pointed nose and gangly limbs.

"Stop stalling, Lorecaster. You're wasting the acolyte's time. Choose, or forfeit your rite," the guard growled, the sound of twisting chains accompanying pain that creased Eldric's face.

"That's enough—" Lorali started.

"Athanasios," Eldric gasped. "I wish to beseech Athanasios for my last rite."

Lorali blinked as a susurrus passed through the crows at the old god's name. The crowd went still and even Sylvene's winds seemed to wait with bated breath to see what would unfold. The god of destruction and chaos wasn't one the people of Athera often prayed to any more. Most did not dare to speak his name in anything above a whisper for fear of inviting him into their space. He was known for his wrath and ire. Many believed that to call upon him in one's last moments was to damn themselves to an eternity within his never-ending chaos.

"*Athanasios.*" Her lips and teeth and tongue formed around the name. It left a sour taste in her mouth as the man before her nodded and she steeled herself to commune with his chosen god.

"Unbind him," Lorali said, unsheathing the dagger she kept tucked within the folds of her robes before holding her own palm skyward. "I'll need his hand."

"I'm sorry, miss, I can't allow an acolyte—"

"That would be *High Cleric Wynmar* to you." Lorali raised her voice, cutting the guard off as her gaze snapped to his, eyes narrowing. He froze, finally noticing her steel bracers inscribed with runes and inlaid with several small stones. A large stellanium jewel rested in the center, glimmering like starlight, as it denoted her station within the Order of Ostara. "And you would be?"

His jaw tensed, as if it took everything within him to bite his tongue. "Fulke, member of the Atheran guard."

"Fulke." Lorali's smile did not reach her eyes, lips pressed together as she continued. "You may not be aware, but in order for me to commune with Athanasios there must be an offering of blood. By law, it is Eldric's right to be given a last prayer to a god of his choosing. Who are you to stand in the way?"

Her chin tilted up, brow raised as she waited. They stood like that for several breaths, a battle of wills, until the guard gave a reluctant nod and a word of warning as he freed one of the prisoner's hands. Eldric rubbed his wrist, reddened by the saw of metal against it. The man rolled his shoulders, as if his arms had been bound behind him for far too long, before placing his calloused hand in her palm. Lorali sent a small prayer to Ostara that she would remember Athanasios' rite she had learned all those years ago, earning the smaller jewels that decorated her bracers.

Ruby blood bloomed as her sharpened dagger bit into their skin. It flowed freely as she pressed their palms together, until it welled onto the ground in soft plops while she began her invocation.

Ice crept through her veins, so unlike the warmth and light she was accustomed to when she connected with her own goddess. It had been seven years since she felt this shivering cold. She had communed with Athanasios for the first and only time when she had branched into connecting with other divinities to better serve the people of the city, earning the smaller jewels that decorated her bracers. No one had asked her to call upon him since.

Lorali's eyes became unseeing as darkness swarmed her vision, ancient words dripping from her lips in whispered prayer. Taking root within her heart as she called his presence forth. The only thing tethering her soul to the soil beneath her feet was the blood offering that continued to trickle to the ground, the warmth of Eldric's hand within her own—a comforting connection to life. She breathed steady and true as a man bathed in the deepest shadows came forth within her mind, his presence alone threatening to dim the very light of her soul.

Lord of shadows, bringer of chaos, ruler of the void—

There is no need for such platitudes, Child of the Star. A voice, cool as night, curled through her mind, making every hair stand on edge. *I know what you seek, and I shall not grant it.*

It was as if his very words had frozen her breath, her heart. Any bit of warmth was sapped in an instant. Her voice trembled as she tried again.

I come on behalf of your devoted—The god wreathed in shadows tilted his head, a chuckle echoing off the corners of her mind.

That boy is no believer of mine. I shall not grant him passage.

Each heartbeat felt like eternity. She opened her mouth, lost at what to say in the face of the god's answer. In all her years, she had never been denied by one of the divine when beseeching them for a blessing for passage into the stars above. She didn't dare let panicked words slip her tongue, lest her own soul be damned.

Not yet, at least, he amended. Though she could not see his features, she could hear the trace of a smile within his voice. *It is not his time. You must guide him, little star, until it is. He will be lost without your light.*

Lorali did her best not to gape at the shadowed figure as their connection flickered once, twice, then dissipated like smoke on the wind without a chance at another word. She did not open her eyes, her body chilled to its core. Needing to collect herself as the god's words replayed in her mind, knowing that the words of ancient beings often held twisted meanings that left more to be discovered.

It is not his time.

Eldric's hand twitched within her own, as if to remind her he was halfway to freedom. That the manacles that suppressed his magic would only work if both wrists were bound to complete the connection. All he had to do was overpower the guard and he would be off once more.

That boy is no believer of mine.

Lorali suppressed an impressed smile. Asking to petition the only god who needed an offering of blood, which required his hands to be freed. Clever boy. She opened her eyes, containing her excitement for whatever was to come. A daring escape by the rogue, eluding the clutches of death once more. Continuing his illegal, though admirable, brand of justice.

It seemed as if the god had approved as well, or else he would not have made Lorali aware of his plans. Her mind raced through the possibilities as she did the god's bidding, leaving events to unfold themselves. She would be protected by the Order should the guard try to blame the escape on her.

"Lord Athanasios has heard your plea, Eldric Lorecaster."

She squeezed his hand tight, fresh blood mingling between their god-chilled palms. Eldric nodded, solemn, and released her hand. The scene unfolded rapidly before Lorali's eyes as Eldric was shackled once more and swiftly escorted up the scaffold, leaving her blinking in stunned silence. He did not fight as he stepped atop the box placed before him, head held high as the canvas sack covered his dark curls, cropped close at the sides. A shiver ran down her spine, and she knew it wasn't residual chills from her petition.

It is not his time.

Athanasios' words lingered along her skin as the guard pronounced Eldric's crimes, from tax evasion to robbery.

It is not his time. You must guide him, little star, until it is.

The necklace of rope draping over him tightened into a knot at the base of his throat. Her hopes withered as realization of what the old god had meant crashed over her in waves.

Eldric Lorecaster didn't have a plan. And neither did she. Instead of silently watching as the thief escaped, the ancient god had entrusted her with the responsibility of keeping him alive. And she was about to fail spectacularly.

"Wait!" she cried, palm outstretched and heart pounding as the guard's hand rested upon the exposed column of Eldric's throat. She hadn't realized she had bolted forward, one foot already on the stairs to the gallows.

"You will release this man at once."

Her mouth spoke before her mind could think, chest trembling and words tumbling out in any attempt to divert Eldric's fate. There was only one thing she could do.

"I, Lorali Wynmar, High Cleric of Ostara, invoke my right to a gallows marriage and claim this man as my husband."

CHAPTER 2

ELDRIC

THE CLERIC'S VOICE CARRIED such command that Fulke stopped, and Eldric couldn't breathe. Not because of the weight of the guard's hand upon his neck or the twisted rope biting into his skin, but from the last kind voice he thought he would ever hear saying the last thing he could have imagined. Words were muffled beneath the canvas hood, but he had heard two of them loud and clear: *gallows marriage.*

Something that only happened in fairytales or books of romance. They weren't real—no cleric had ever made the offering in his lifetime. To enter a gallows marriage was to entrust your life to the one at the end of the rope. A promise before the gods to reform the person you saved, or forfeit your own life if you failed.

The noose loosened and the crowd roared—cheers and curses both filling the square as it slipped from his neck while the cleric and the guardsman argued. Fulke ripped the hood from his face and Eldric breathed in the crisp air, blinking into the bright, overcast sky. He couldn't focus on their words, senses flooding back with overwhelming force. Knees buckling beneath him, Eldric toppled over. He couldn't help but notice the swirling wood grain beneath him as he coughed, hands still bound behind his back.

"Do you accept?" the cleric questioned; frustration was clear in the way her brows creased together, as if she had asked the question more times than she cared to and was still waiting for an answer. Her small frame should have been dwarfed by the tall construct that was the gallows, but somehow, she stood tall. Occupying more space than she logically could have, even with her firm stance and fists placed upon her hips.

"Do I—"

"Accept the offer of a gallows bond, a chance at redemption for your crimes."

Eldric had never been a man of faith; most of what he knew of the gods and goddesses was in the form of forgotten hymns and prayers learned in childhood. He glanced at the constellation of stars embroidered along the shoulders of her deep blue cloak and his stomach twisted into more knots than he could imagine. His tongue ran across his dry, cracked lips as he looked around him and weighed his options.

"Do I even have a choice?"

"Yes." The cleric blinked up at him, unfazed. "It's this, or death. I assume you'd prefer the former."

A half-choked laugh escaped him at her boldness, pulling his gaze back down to study her. So matter-of-fact, so calm, as if saving people from death's door was a normal occurrence. Perhaps it was—the life of a cleric was unknown to him.

Eldric's head tilted, watching the woman before him. He wondered if her heart was pounding as fast as his was now. "When you put it that way..." he hummed, feeling rage roiling off Fulke as he pretended to deliberate. "I accept."

"Perfect," she said, eyes narrowing in the guard's direction with a wave of her hand. *Free him*, she commanded without a word. Eldric bit back a yelp of pain as the guard yanked the chains binding his shackles together and pulled him to stand.

"You're lucky she has a bleeding heart," Fulke hissed. The sound of the key sliding home into the shackles could be heard above his voice as it turned once, then twice. It was the sound of freedom that had Eldric breathing the smallest sigh of relief. His chest trembled as he glanced through the crowd, and scanned the tops of the surrounding buildings. Disappointment burned in the back of his throat as he failed to find his closest friend. He had thought that Daeson, before anyone else, would have saved him.

"Sorry to disappoint, Fulke. You'll have to fantasize about someone else's death now that I'm under the protection of the Order." Eldric hoped his smirk didn't falter as he rolled his wrist. His heart pounded, head rushing. Standing on the box and feeling the rope cut into his skin—death had been too close.

"I have no worries, Lorecaster. You'll be back with that pretty little cleric at your side soon enough. Poor girl doesn't know the mistake she's made putting her faith in you. An oathbreaker like you will never change."

Anger flashed through Eldric, his hands moving before his mind could register the fistful of Fulke's shirt within them. Eyes blazing, magic sparking to life. The guard sneered, knowing he'd struck a nerve. Their voices raised, fighting for dominance over each other before the cleric's commanding voice cut through them both, strong enough to make them freeze.

"*Enough!*"

He didn't know how she managed to look down on them with disapproval when she was ten feet below them, but she did. It was the disapproval only a holy person could muster.

"Stop provoking him or I will have you taken to tribunal for obstruction of the Order," she said, admonishing Fulke as if he were a child. Eldric couldn't help the snicker that escaped him as he watched the vein running across the guard's forehead bulge as he ground his teeth.

Protection, Eldric mouthed.

"And you—" she continued, turning on Eldric as he released the fistfuls of fabric. Her eyes simmered with uncertainty, lips pressing together as she searched for her words. "Get down here. Don't make me regret this."

Eldric's palms faced outward as he stepped back toward the stairs, silently making his way down the scaffold. He didn't want to tempt fate further, fearing she would change her mind and he would have to feel the weight of his body send him to his death.

"Our binding will be within the temple at first light," the cleric declared as Eldric came to her side, Fulke following close at his heels. She sidestepped the thief, standing between him and his guard with her chin tilted upwards in defiance. "Bring your commander."

Fulke fumed, pulling his shoulders back to appear larger—more intimidating. It made Eldric's skin crawl, sitting wrong within his bones having another person defend him. He almost pushed her away, took his rightful place in the path of Fulke's fury, but he saw the set of her jaw and knew she wouldn't allow it.

"You will regret this," the guardsman seethed. "If you were smart, this is the last man you would take in a gallows marriage. He will break his oath to you as well. Next time, you should research the man you're saving before enacting your romantic fantasies. Not that there will be a next time."

"Are you done?" she asked, crossing her arms.

A growl ripped itself from Fulke's throat as he pushed forward, knocking the cleric's shoulder as he stormed off.

Eldric could have sworn he heard her curse him beneath her breath as she shook her head. She gave a sigh, pinching between her brows as if he were the greatest headache she had ever encountered. Her clear grey eyes were scrunched as she shook her head with a muttered prayer, her light hair framing her face in delicate tendrils. He watched as she rolled her shoulders back, standing tall as she extended her hand. Even with the braided coronet woven across her head, she didn't come to his chin.

"Lorali Wynmar, High Cleric of Ostara," she said. Her small frame looked as if he could toss her over his shoulder with ease, or that a strong wind might take her. But the steel bracers he had noticed when their blood-soaked hands were clasped said this was a woman formidable in her own right. That if the Order had not claimed her, she would have been a force for change in the world.

"My... wife?" Eldric hesitated on the word, watching the way color rose high in her freckle-smattered cheeks as the wind blew stray hairs into her face.

"Not yet, but soon to be," she said, brushing the hairs away when he didn't take her hand. Lorali took his forearm instead and pulled him behind her. "Follow me. We have much to discuss."

It was not a question.

She wove through the crowd with expert ease, dragging him behind, and leaving Eldric to apologize in her wake. They quickly made their way out of the crowded square and through the back alley. Neither of them said anything to break the silence as they continued to walk toward the edge of the city. He said nothing, instead monitoring his surroundings closely. Looking for any sign that they were being followed by Fulke or someone else deciding to take what they believed to be justice into their own hands. His hopeful gaze mistaking every set of inky hair and dark eyes amongst the crowd for Daeson.

The scent of herb-crusted meats and root vegetables wafted through the air, and when the cleric's stomach growled so loud it caught even his attention, he couldn't help the chuckle that escaped. "You sound hungrier than me, and I haven't eaten in days."

"Days?" she asked.

"Why waste food on those you're planning to execute?" he responded, voice grim.

Her pale lips tipped downward, eyes scanning every vendor along the road until she found one that caught her attention.

"We should eat," she said, inclining her head toward a rough lean-to propped against a wall. Eldric's mouth watered at the thought of food, but he froze as she ordered two roasted potatoes spiraled onto a stick. It was a questionable place to eat at best, a place he would get a bad case of food sickness from at the worst. Compared to the other overwhelming and savory smells filling the crowded streets, the meager lean-to was the least impressive stall.

When Lorali held out one of the spiraled vegetables to him, it took everything within him not to immediately grab it.

"I don't have money," he said, unable to help the way his mouth watered as the smell of butter and spring onions from the neighboring flatbread stall made his own stomach growl in response. He doubted he should start off whatever their little agreement was with stealing his own food, but he was close to doing just that if he wasn't removed from the temptation.

"I didn't ask if you had money to pay." She shook her head, holding out the skewer towards him. "I said we should eat. Now take it."

Eldric blinked, looking to the questionable vendor behind her, then back to the food before him. He would gladly take anything, even poorly seasoned, if it meant satisfying the pit within his stomach. He took a bite, a groan escaping as he savored the subtle flavor of dried herbs mixed with the crisp roasted potato. Then again, who was he to judge a man's cooking capabilities based on his facilities? He was a convict, a crook.

Oathbreaker, Fulke had called him.

That word pierced his heart. Burned like acid and he tried to shove it down with every bite as they walked in relative silence, filled only by the sounds of their footsteps and the crunch of food.

"A thank you would be nice," Lorali finally said, breaking their silence.

"For this?" He waved the half-eaten potato in his hand.

"Yes, the potato. Of course." Sarcasm dripped from every word. "I saved you."

"I never asked you to."

"You were going to die."

Eldric shrugged, taking another bite. "And what if I was okay with that?"

Lorali did not falter in her questioning. "Did you want to die?"

"Does it matter now?"

He continued to eat his potato in blessed silence when she didn't respond, following her wherever she was leading him. He could run, damning her to deal with the consequences for letting him escape. But what Fulke said was stuck beneath his skin, a splinter wedging itself deeper until it was all he could feel. Unable to move forward until it was removed.

"What if your soul would not have been granted passage?" she asked.

"I didn't choose to have you petition Athanasios due to his sunny disposition." Eldric snorted, shaking his head. He looked to the woman at his side as they ascended the stone stairs up the hillside. "This seems like an unfair amount of one-sided questioning."

"I don't hear you asking any questions, now do I?" She picked a spiral of potato and tore it off the skewer instead of biting straight into it as he had.

"Why?"

"Why what? Why am I eating my potato like this?" she hedged. Eldric snorted.

"Yes, that is certainly a curiosity of mine."

"I look like less of a fool when eating," she said, placing a finger between her lips and savoring the residual spices.

They walked in silence again, Lorali picking at her potato and Eldric having long since discarded his empty skewer in the nearest bin. Neither of them discussed the question sitting heavy within his chest as the houses became sparse and trees began to rise from the ground, blocking the sunlight and casting shadows that grew long as the sun continued to sink low in the sky.

Lorali fished a set of keys out from beneath her robes as they neared the end of the street. They entered a yard with its small, lush garden just beginning to grow on either side. Ivy climbed high across the stucco and stone, growing wild and embedding itself into the chimney. As she unlocked the door, lights began to flicker on within the home. He stood, rooted to the spot. Could not take another step without knowing.

"Why did you save me?"

Her shoulders tensed as she turned to face him.

"That—" her voice wavered for the first time since he had met her. She pressed her lips together, standing in the large maple doorway that towered above her.

"That is something we talk about over drinks."

CHAPTER 3

LORALI

HOT TEA IN HAND, Eldric had taken the near loss of his soul quite well. The steaming cup of home-grown lavender and chamomile and rose, sweetened with a dash of honeyed whiskey, likely helped to take the edge off. Lorali was sure he needed it just as much, if not more, than she did right now.

"If Athanasios said it wasn't my time, why didn't you say anything sooner?" he asked, watching small bits of flowers that snuck through the strainer swirl around the mushroom-adorned mug.

"I thought you had a plan," Lorali admitted as she fidgeted with the deep green stoneware, rubbing the divots and grooves of the embossed forest design.

"Athanasios is the only god that requires a blood offering. When he said you were no follower of his, I thought it was a ploy to free your hands. Why else would someone beseech him? As you said before, he is not known for his, ah, *sunny disposition.*" She whispered, leaning in as if speaking quietly would not allow the old god to hear her.

"I've heard much about you, Eldric Lorecaster. You have to be cunning—clever, even—to be a thief of such caliber and only be caught now. I presumed you would not give up so easily." Her brows knit together as she searched for the truth in the bottom of her tea. "But when you didn't put up a fight and Fulke put those shackles back on you, I panicked. I realized too late that Athanasios had charged me with keeping you from death. A gallows marriage was the only thing I could think of to stop it. To not fail what he had tasked me with."

"And now we're here," Eldric said.

"And now we're here," Lorali agreed.

"I could leave, you know. Run off into the night and leave you to deal with the consequences."

"I know." Her grip tightened on the mug, crafted antlers of a stag pressing into her skin. "But I don't think you will."

Eldric blew out a breath as he leaned back, holding his mug precariously by the rim. His long limbs looked crowded in the small chair as he stretched out. "Now why on Ostara's lighted soil would you think that?"

She worried her bottom lip, thinking of her heartbeat decision. How little thought she had put into it. "I have to believe that someone who would steal from nobles to care for and feed the hungry people of this city would be a man of honor."

Lorali clutched her cup tighter, so tight she thought it might break, as a humorless chuckle escaped his lips.

"A man of honor..." Eldric shook his head in disbelief as he reached for the honeyed whiskey, topping off his half-drunken mug. "It's been a long time since someone has thought so highly of me."

"Am I wrong?"

"Depends who you ask."

"Is that why Fulke called you an oathbreaker?"

Eldric stilled at the words, gaze sharp on hers in an instant.

"Yes, it is. I *am* an oathbreaker. Far from a man of honor, Miss Wynmar. And before you ask, since you never seem to know when to stop asking: no, I will not divulge further." His words were short and clipped as he drank deeply from his now-mostly-whiskey tea. He set it down with such force that Lorali couldn't help but flinch. Silence settled heavy between them. He wasn't wrong; she would have pushed him further. She wanted to know everything she could about him. Needed to, for the sake of her own sanity.

"Miss Wynmar—" she drawled after a prolonged silence, trying to get back on his good side. The last thing she wanted was to start whatever journey they were about to embark upon together on the wrong foot. "Does that mean you intend to take my last name then? Or shall I be taking the name Lorecaster?"

"We keep our own names," he growled. "Despite the ceremony tomorrow, I am not bound to you. This isn't a genuine marriage. You look like you can't be over eighteen. It would never work, darling."

She couldn't help the small grin that quirked the edge of her mouth at his quick quip.

"Twenty-six. And I'm glad we're on the same page."

"What?"

"I'm twenty-six."

Eldric's brows rose at that.

"Twenty-six? What do you take me for, a fool?"

"Believe what you want, but I take care of my skin. That way I don't look old and haggard when I'm over forty like you," she bit back.

"*Over forty?*" he repeated incredulously.

"You're too old for me—it would never work between us." She crooned.

"I'm thirty-two, I'll have you know."

"Your grey hairs say otherwise."

He gaped, hand flying to the close-cropped sides as if to cover the truth.

"I'm observant," she smiled. "So, as we were agreeing, this 'marriage' is a formality, though we will have to abide by the rules of the bond. One year of good behavior and you'll officially be a freed man."

"Cheeky little shit," he grumbled.

"Much of what is known about the gallows bond is lost to antiquity, so we'll have to live together while we figure things out. For now, you can have the couch—which is rather comfortable, truth be told. I must clean the spare bedroom before you can sleep in there."

Lorali continued as if he'd said nothing, prattling off like a commander going to battle as she took the teapot and her mug to the sink.

"I won't interfere with your daily life if you stay out of mine. I'll have to do more research on what the bond entails. It's unfortunate that there isn't much information out there in official texts..." she muttered with a frown, dumping the tea strainings into her bin before turning the faucet on.

"Aye, commander," Eldric muttered, cheek resting against his palm. "Traded one warden for another."

"What'd you say?" Lorali whirled on him with a raised eyebrow, feeling as if she might throw her favourite mug at this head.

"Nothing, dear," he responded in a sing-song voice before returning to nurse his drink in silence.

She narrowed her eyes, certain he said something cross about her but unsure of what over the sound of running water.

"That's what I thought."

CHAPTER 4

ELDRIC

THEY WERE UP BEFORE the sun, walking down the narrow and winding streets to the temple in sleepy morning silence. Lorali had been right—the couch was more comfortable than he thought it'd be. It still didn't help him sleep more than an hour throughout the night. His body was too wired, mind running too fast as he stared at the dark wood ceiling beams wondering just what he had agreed to. His soon-to-be wife was in no better shape, dark circles beneath her eyes as she folded a colorful piece of fabric and tucked it into her satchel.

"Not getting cold feet, are we?" he asked, tone light as he tried to find some sense of normalcy in their very abnormal day. She glared at him, pouring her brew into a mug that she held onto throughout their journey. Curling into the crisp morning air, the steam from the mug mingled with her breath. If he hadn't provoked her so early, maybe she would have extended the offer of a cup to him too.

The temple's high spires towered over them in the darkness, shadows thrown high from the flickering street lanterns. His pace slowed, feet rooting him within the looming darkness. A shiver that had nothing to do with the morning chill crawled along his spine. After a few steps, Lorali stopped—hesitating before the door as she turned back to find him rooted in place. Despite her fatigue, her eyes were sharp. Studying the stiffness in his stance, the hesitation in his glance. Reading him as if he were a book.

"Ever been to the Order's temple?" she asked, speaking for the first time since they left the cottage. Her voice was soothing, a balm against his nerves. He tried his best to shake the tension from his shoulders as he followed her through the unfamiliar side entrance.

"Once," he breathed, "long ago."

"It's not as scary on the inside, promise," she said with a small smile before devouring the last of her drink and setting her mug on a nearby windowsill. And to her, perhaps it wasn't. She seemed genuine—good even. In the half a day he'd known her, he'd felt at ease despite their strange situation. She'd welcomed him into her home and showed him kindness with no expectation of it in return. He wondered if she would think so highly of the Order if she knew what secrets lurked within it. It twisted something in his gut to think that she could know, and still choose to be a follower.

He was thankful that his guide was not the chatty sort. It gave him time to observe as they navigated through the warren that was the temple, memorizing the twists and turns as they went. He watched how her steps quickened as they neared the center. They entered the massive room filled with empty pews and soaring stained glass through a side door. He couldn't help the way his footsteps stopped as his eyes followed the walls up, up, and *up*—until they reached the high domed ceiling capped in pure glass, letting the fading stars shine through. It was as marvelous as he remembered.

"My, my, my—I can't believe the day has come where I see my little Lorali married. And through a gallows bond, no less," a male voice called playfully.

Eldric flinched, unable to identify where the voice was coming from. Lorali's steps did not falter as she gave an exasperated sigh.

"I'm not your 'little' anything, Heinrich. Stop being nosey—your presence isn't required."

"Someone hasn't had their morning brew," Heinrich chuckled as he popped up from a pew he had been laying on. "And oh, how you are wrong, Lor. My presence is

absolutely required. Who would give you away to this...
upstanding citizen, if not I?"

"I am not something to be given away, Heinrich." Lorali bristled, mild annoyance flickering across her face as she crossed her arms. "It may be a tradition, but it is not required by any means."

Heinrich's cheerful voice turned serious as he leaned over the pew when they neared. His dark skin stood out against the light wood even in the flickering lowlight of freshly lit candles. The man's grey eyes, so similar to Lorali's, glanced at him.

"Trust me, you want me here. You're all anyone has been talking about since that guard barged in with his commander yesterday. You proposed a gallows marriage to one of the most wanted men in the city, then proceeded to inform the archcleric by phoenix letter rather than, oh I don't know, telling us in person?" Heinrich groaned, dragging his hands down his face. "The city council is furious; the guard is saying he paid you to do this. Bribery, Lor. That's an excommunicable *and* executable offense."

Lorali stopped at the pew before him, her shoulders drawn back and chin held high. "I did not accept any bribe."

"Hello, upstanding citizen here," Eldric said with a small wave. "Can confirm that she, in fact, wasn't bribed. Not by me anyway."

"Not helping," she shot back without missing a beat.

"What on this lighted earth were you thinking to pull such an ancient trick, Lor? I mean, he is a looker, but his reputation is less than desirable." Heinrich's eyes slowly traveled from Eldric's dirty boots all the way up to his messy curls.

"Bite me," Eldric grumbled, shifting from foot to foot beneath the man's gaze as he stood beside Lorali with crossed arms.

"Don't tempt him," Lorali warned.

Heinrich chuckled at that, a smirk showing that maybe, just maybe, he might.

"Sage had to assure the council that they would personally oversee your binding and that you would be kept close to the Order throughout your bonded year."

Lorali bit her lip, closing her eyes as she took a steadying breath through her nose. "Shit."

"Yeah, shit indeed. Sage was already not happy about you communing with other deities."

"It's been years; you'd think they'd be over it by now," she grumbled.

"Not when their protégée high cleric foiled their plans to make her the next archcleric. That's why you've been on gallows duty ever since. They're hoping you'll give it up."

Eldric coughed with surprise. "Archcleric?"

"Don't ask, Lorecaster," Lorali snapped.

"You're full of surprises, *Lor*." The nickname rolled off the rogue's tongue with ease as he grinned.

"Oh yes, your wife-to-be is quite the accomplished cleric for one so young," Heinrich said wistfully, standing as the door opened. "Look alive, you two," he continued with a nod to the back of the nave. Through the door, the sun was just beginning to crest over the hill, painting the sky in swathing shades of orange.

Fulke's gangly silhouette was accompanied by someone much taller and much broader. A mountain of a man with the city's crest embroidered over his heart—a symbol of his unwavering loyalty to law and order.

"Commander Sorin," Eldric greeted tightly, standing straighter as the Commander of the Atheran Guard neared. As if it would make him feel any more at ease in his presence. He only spared Fulke a withering glance. The guard sneered but said nothing in the presence of his superior.

"Eldric," he replied with a curt nod.

"A pleasure to see you again, sir," Lorali said with her hand outstretched in greeting. Commander Sorin's hand enveloped her own, dwarfing her already petite hand into obscurity within his black-gloved clasp.

"Likewise..." the commander started but struggled to remember a name.

"Lorali," she supplied with an awkward laugh, scratching the back of her head. "It's been a while—we met back when you were still a captain."

"Ah, right," the commander nodded in agreement, reticent and wearing his usual stern expression.

"Sage will be here shortly, Commander," Heinrich said, stepping in and guiding Commander Sorin and Fulke away from the pair with ease. "They're cleansing to allow proper communion with the gods. Allow me to bless you in the meantime before the nuptials."

As quickly as they entered, they were corralled away.

"Sorin's awful with names, don't take it personally," Eldric whispered, his hand touching her shoulder as he leaned in, nodding toward Heinrich who was praying over the guards. "Do we have to do that?"

"No, Heinrich just likes to show off," Lorali said with a snort.

"So... Archcleric?" Eldric pestered.

"That's—" she shook her head with a scoff. "You know what? No. If you get to have secrets from me, I get to keep mine from you."

"Yes, miss former-next-archcleric," he teased with a chuckle. He was surprised when Lorali grabbed his wrist and squeezed it tight, pulling him in close enough that their noses nearly touched.

"Do not breathe a word of that to anyone. Heinrich shouldn't know, let alone be telling anyone. Especially outside the faith," she whispered, deathly calm. Her clear grey eyes bore into his own and he couldn't help the tilt to his head as he leaned in.

"Well, I am your husband-to-be," Eldric crooned into her ear. "My lips are sealed."

He couldn't help but notice the way her jaw tensed and her ears blushed a delicate shade of pink beneath his whispers. Their little game of banter from the previous night had brought him joy, and he was sure that over the next year they would find new ways to tease each other. Delight filled him at the thought, a lazy grin spreading as he gazed down at her defiant stare.

A throat clearing caught their attention and they sprung apart in an instant, as if they were conspirators caught by surprise.

"High Cleric Wynmar," called a mild voice from the pulpit. "It has been an age."

"Archcleric Sage," Lorali said, bowing deeply. Heinrich and the guards did the same. Eldric stood firm, not bowing until Lorali yanked him down with her.

"May the goddess shine upon you," she and Heinrich intoned in near unison.

"And upon you," replied the archcleric. Lorali allowed Eldric to rise with her. Sage stood before them, flowing robes obscuring their form. Eldric recognized that ageless face, neither feminine nor masculine, that just was. Long silver hair framed grey eyes that glimmered with hidden knowledge, ears that ended in a short point sticking out. It made every hair on his body stand on edge, skin prickling as they spoke.

"I see your propensity for commotion has not changed." Sage smiled down at them and though it was not kind, it held no malice either.

"I strive to live my life by Ostara's guiding light as her humble servant," Lorali replied, her hand still on his wrist. He wondered if she could feel his quickening pulse beneath her fingertips.

Sage's smile grew taut as they nodded, clasping their hands together—the sound echoing loudly off the stone and colored glass inlaid within it.

"Let us move forward with the binding. I'm sure we all have plenty else to do with this day."

Lorali nodded, pulling that colorful piece of fabric from home out of her satchel before stepping forward, her hand still on Eldric's wrist. He was tired of being dragged along by the wrist as if he were a child and slid his hand into hers as she pulled him toward the pulpit. Whether because she didn't care or didn't notice, Lorali didn't fight him. The soft morning glow of first light began filtering in from above, that time between night and day hanging in a delicate balance as they stood before the archcleric.

"Which god did you petition for his rite?" Sage inquired, taking the fabric. Their gaze never left Lorali's and never acknowledged Eldric's existence. She hesitated, the god's name hanging on her lips as if she were afraid to speak it in the archcleric's presence.

"Athanasios," Eldric supplied in her stead.

Lorali's fingers twitched against Eldric's, her grip tightening around his beneath the weight of Sage's disapproving gaze.

"Of course." That false smile dipped downward, pure distaste spreading across their features. "This is why you shouldn't be communing with other gods, Lorali. They put you into unsavory situations that the Mother of Stars would never dare. Heinrich, the salts—we must keep this contained. We don't want the god of chaos desecrating Ostara's temple."

Lorali's eyes were downcast, mouth set into a firm line as Sage stepped away and her friend took a pitcher from a low cabinet, beginning to pour a thick salt line. It followed the outline of the skylight, encircling and separating them from others within the room.

"You'll feel him this time," she whispered to Eldric as she pushed her sleeves back and unbandaged her palm, revealing her wound that matched his own. He followed her movements, wordlessly revealing the pink and scabbed-over gash as she unsheathed her dagger. "It will be as cold as death, but I am with you. Always. You are safe with me, just don't let go."

Without warning, she reopened their freshly healed wounds with an archer's precision, blood flowing between their joined hands. The archcleric took the length of fabric, wrapping it around their hands with expert precision and taking extra care not to soil their pristine clothes. Maroon began to seep through the fabric binding them together.

"Begin," was all Sage said as they looked down at Lorali and Eldric.

Lorali took that steadying breath of hers, the one he'd noticed she took when she was preparing herself, as she began her petition to the god of shadows once more. Eldric stiffened as his vision faded to nothingness; he only saw Lorali burning brighter than flame before him, their joined hands remaining warm as the rest of his blood ran cold and dark.

Lord Athanasios, Lorali spoke, voice resounding within his mind. Within his very soul.

The nothingness took form and moved, sitting upon a dark throne painted in varying shades of darkness before them.

No honeyed words for me this time, little star? the old god drawled.

You said there was no need for platitudes.

Eldric stilled at her brazen words. Was that how one was supposed to speak to a god? The ruler of chaos itself? Considering the circumstances, he determined that it would be in his best interest to keep his lips sealed and leave the talking to Lorali. The last thing he wanted was to anger the god who had decided, for one reason or another, to have his life spared.

That I did. The god's voice seemed to curl into a smile, bemused at the pair before him as his head rested against his knuckles. To Eldric's utter shock he seemed pleased. He didn't know how she could stand there beneath the overwhelming pressure of death and even think. But she did, her hand tight around his own.

I did as you asked.

In the most interesting of ways, it seems.

The shadows turned toward Eldric and he felt pure terror overtake him beneath the god's gaze. It took everything within him not to tremble. Lorali squeezed her hand around his, a reassurance. As if knowing what he felt and reminding him she was there. She had promised him he was safe within her light.

Luck must have been on your side when you beseeched me, child. Any other god would have left you to the noose. You can call it a benefit of my sunny disposition, if you will.

Lorali stiffened at the familiar words. Eldric swallowed, that feeling of biting rope against his skin and the fear of impending darkness still fresh within his mind. He feared it could turn into reality at any moment the god pleased.

Thank you, he said with lips pressed tightly together.

I am not the one deserving of thanks, boy. That would be owed to your guiding star. The darkness nodded to Lorali. *But we have little time to waste, as I grow tired of your archcleric's attempts to interfere. Face each other so we may begin the ceremony.*

While the god drew nearer, they complied with the command. Eldric's other hand found hers, the feel of her palm against his own providing a sense of reassurance. She had promised that he would be safe. He repeated the thought to himself over and over again—those eyes full of confidence and hope had not betrayed him yet. Something within him believed they wouldn't. A cold hand settled upon their shoulders, the god's voice resonating in a forgotten tongue that sent cold flame into his very bones.

He clenched his teeth, eyes slamming shut. Only able to feel the onslaught of pain berating his senses. The god's touch drew a scream from him, his flesh burning with the brightest pain he had ever known, stealing every bit of heat from his body. Lorali's grip on him tightened with a whimper. Her nails biting into his skin were nothing compared to that scorching pain. It crept through his arm toward their bloody palms; toward the only piece of warmth that still existed within him. He feared it might go out, taking him and her under with it. That he had postponed his death, but only so long. But the warmth did not sputter or waver beneath the god's magic, holding steady as a flame between them.

As the god stepped back, it left Eldric gasping, eyes flying open—the lack of sensation as painful as the onslaught he had just experienced. He blinked at Lorali's tearstained face, following her gaze to their joined hands now inked with the same winding black design. His gaze followed the pattern from the thick black band on her third finger swirling up her arm until it was hidden beneath her sleeve, matching his own.

Now that you are bound, you must not be far from each other. Your lives are interwoven; what happens to one happens to both, including death. Do not let it happen, boy. The god's voice was almost accusatory, as if he knew that between the two, Eldric would be the most likely cause.

Understood, was all he could manage.

Seal your bond, then, and be off. I will see you soon, little star. Remember who your light burns for. It will guide the way for you both.

Thank you for your wisdom, Lord Athanasios. Lorali's voice was strained and hollow as she bowed her head to the god.

Eldric looked down at her, confused. Seal their bond? What could that possibly—

He did not have to wonder any longer as Lorali's hand that was not tethering them to their world reached forward and grasped his collar, pulling his lips down into an earth-shattering kiss.

CHAPTER 5

LORALI

LORALI PRESSED THE SPARE metal key into Eldric's palms, curling his fingers over it as she sent him off from the small side room they'd entered that morning. Her hands didn't shake, but her throat was tight as she bit her lower lip nervously. They were testing the limits of their bond—how far could it be pulled and bent? What were its limits? They'd have to discover for themselves.

"What if one of us is suffering the consequences, but the other isn't?" Eldric murmured, still dazed from his encounter with Lord Athanasios.

"I'll come home, or you'll come here. We'll find each other," she said with more confidence than she felt.

"I could..." his voice trailed off, hesitating.

"Stay here?" Lorali shook her head. "Do you want to be at my side for the next year? We don't know the rules—we'll have to push until we break them to find out. See what we can tolerate."

Eldric winced as he pocketed the key. "I'd rather not relive that pain ever again if I can help it."

"I know," she agreed, lips pressed tight together. "We won't let it get that bad."

Planning was the only thing they could do in the face of the unknown. She couldn't stand the thought of not knowing the limits of their new arrangement. She tried to reassure him, reaching out tentatively to touch his arm, but retracted the hand hastily.

"We'll figure this out," she promised. "It will be okay. But I have to go now. I—"

Eldric's jaw tightened, his voice strained. "Right. Summoned by the archcleric."

Lorali nodded, turning to leave before Eldric reached forward and grabbed her hand.

"Don't be too late," he said. Her heart stuttered, a small flicker of warm flame passing between their joined hands, those matching markings they had received from the dark god branded upon their physical forms.

"I'll try," she said, despite knowing she couldn't keep that kind of promise. The Order came first, always. She turned, passing through the door and making her way toward the archcleric's study. After a few heartbeats, she felt like a tether between them was being pulled taut. Pulling her chest in his direction. As if her heart was walking away with him.

***

The temple's basement was dark, lit only by the steady, cool light of the lucernas ensconced upon the wall like jewels mixing with flickering candles surrounding her desk. Her mind switched between research on the gallows bond and her ideas for Veridian, unable to stay focused on one task for long before her attention was pulled. She was isolated from any hint of sunlight and only the sound of pages flipping filled the silence.

Despite the ache that crept into her chest, she pushed through to focus on her work. Determined to ignore how she felt tugged in one direction, called to follow the pull so she could rid herself of the dull throb that settled within her. She knew it was the bond. Throwing herself into her work, she would do anything to keep her unfocused mind away from places it did not need to wander.

She did not think about how they had sealed the bond. Could not think about how it had severed their connection to the dark god's realm, returning warmth to their bodies. Would not think about how Eldric's arm pulled her closer or the way he had kissed her back like she was air and he the flame. Lorali dropped her burning face into her hands and shut her eyes tight, pushing any such thoughts to the farthest edges of her mind.

"Don't want to spend time with your husband for the honeymoon?" Heinrich called, bearing gifts of soft cheese and fresh bread to fuel her studies. She couldn't help but smile at the spoonful of red pepper jam he had stuffed onto the side of the small plate for her, knowing it was her favourite. A sigh escaped her lips as she held out her hands for the offering from her friend with a smile. It was the first food she had seen all day, too focused on her studies to move from the spot she had sat in for the last several hours. Her stomach growled in protest of its starvation.

"We may be bonded, but we are not actually married, Hein."

"That kiss said otherwise." He raised an eyebrow, turning the seat across from her backwards and draping himself over the back of the chair, fanning himself mockingly. "Even I was getting hot and bothered by it. That man looks like he'd be an excellent—"

Lorali slammed the book shut, her chest rising and falling as color rose to her cheeks. *"And we're done with this conversation."*

Lorali picked apart her bread, spreading the soft cheese and topping it with the jam before savoring her first bite. Heinrich's expression softened as he stopped his fun.

"I'm just saying, Lor, this might not be a bad thing. Unconventional, yes, but not necessarily bad. You've been alone, stars, the entire time I've known you. Even if it's not romantic. Having some kind of partner outside of the Order is more of a blessing than you even realize. It gives you perspective, helps you grow and learn."

"There's a reason high clerics don't often have connections outside the Order," she said slowly. "We're overworked and constantly absorbed in our duties. An outsider would never understand. While we may be bonded, that doesn't mean we owe each other anything."

"He owes you everything. More than he can ever repay," Heinrich said, bristling. "You saved him, gave him a second chance at life, are opening your home and your life to him."

"And did I ever ask him if that was what he wanted?" she asked. Tears stung behind her eyes and her throat tightened as her worries bubbled their way to the surface. She felt that tug in her chest once more, as if their bond needed to remind her it was there. "No, I made an impulsive decision and dragged him into this mess. He would never have chosen this if I hadn't forced his hand."

"You saved a man's life, yet you make it sound like it was something selfish." Heinrich's gaze softened, his pale palms enveloping her hands with a squeeze. Lorali fell quiet at that, eyes fixed on the candle flame before her as she tried to keep the tears at bay. Silence settled between them once more and they stayed like that, in comfort.

"Do you think he deserved to die?" he finally asked, voice hesitant.

Her throat bobbed and eyes closed as she shook her head. Unable to give voice to her thoughts. She thought that the Order and the guard were wrong to put him to death. He had only ever served Athera, in his own way, when the city's council wouldn't. Heinrich was the only one she could ever confess this to. He smiled, knowing.

"Neither did I," he whispered. "I'm glad you saved him, and I'm sure many others in the city are as well. Don't use your good deed as an excuse to tear yourself down, okay?"

Lorali nodded with a sigh as he patted her hand.

"Congratulations on being chosen as the Sun Bearer, by the way," Heinrich said. "What an exciting day for you—got yourself a husband *and* a promotion."

Lorali's questioning gaze snapped to his. It hadn't been even an hour since she left the archcleric's office where she'd been appointed as the next Sun Bearer—charged with organizing the next Veridian celebration and guiding

Ostara back with the growing sun come next spring. It was a massive undertaking that would keep her, and Eldric, close to the Order for the next year.

To be chosen was to devote oneself wholly to Ostara, requiring immense and meticulous preparation. It was one of the highest honors bestowed within the Order, one she had only dreamed of receiving. Now the opportunity tasted sour, as if it were given to her out of necessity rather than deserved.

She couldn't help her faint smile at his antics, though, knowing he was trying to lift her spirits. "How'd you know?"

"I know everything that goes on within the Order, Lorali. You know that by now," he said with a wicked grin, eyes gleaming in the lowlight as he sat back. "I think you will host one of the greatest Veridian celebrations of our time."

"Better than yours?" she teased.

"Better than mine," he said in earnest.

Together, Lorali and Heinrich worked in tireless tandem to research and begin the first stages of planning. They worked until the sun fell and the moon rose and the stars shone bright overhead, unaware of it all in the windowless basement. Time passed only in candles burnt to waxy puddles, cooling and sticking to the whorls of wood grain.

Heinrich finally forced her to leave, knowing she didn't have the power to stop herself from continuing on to her own detriment. The trek to her house had never felt so far, that dull throb from before having turned into a full pounding that demanded attention. She knew the path home, but even if she had been blind she would have been able to follow the pull of the tether that was leading her to him.

She walked up the path to her cottage, the loam dormant as winter ended and spring began. Unlocking the door, she stumbled into the house, tripping over his muddy boots.

"It's about time you showed up."

Eldric's voice carried from the kitchen along with the mouthwatering scent of savory onions and pungent garlic mixed with herbs and earthy mushrooms.

"I know, I'm sorry," she apologized, kicking off her shoes before making her way to the kitchen. He had made himself at home in her cottage, finding pots and pans she rarely used since she often ate food at the temple. "You cook?"

"You get good at it when you're trying to avoid the law. Needed something to distract myself from this torture you've subjected me to today," he said as he took a bottle of her favourite wine and poured it into the sizzling pan, scraping up the brown bits into the sauce. A sound of protest died in her throat as he kept talking. "You don't have a lot of food here, which is saying something coming from me, but I made do."

"You're awfully judgmental for someone who is cooking with someone else's food," she grumbled. "How about some apology tea? Maybe it'll help alleviate the pain," she offered, already moving to gather her ingredients.

"You could call it apolo-*tea*?" he hedged, making her groan. Eldric chuckled as he turned back to the wood fire stove.

"I'd be delighted to have more of that brew from yester-day."

"Sure, let me just grab—" Lorali turned to the cupboard that held her small collection of mugs, dismayed as she opened it and realized she'd forgotten—"my mug. How did...?"

She blinked, her favourite forest green mug sitting fresh-ly washed in the cupboard. Picking it up, she turned it over carefully in her hands, feeling the weight of it, the familiar grooves and divots pressing into her hand. She could have sworn she'd forgotten it at the temple.

"You left it in the windowsill by the door we came in. Thought you might forget it, so I grabbed it on my way out."

She stood, speechless. Marveling at the mug as if she had not used it faithfully for the last five years. The amount of times she had left it was embarrassing.

"Thank you," she said, a small smile tugging at her lips. She had been right—a man of honor. No matter how he might try to deny it, there was a good person beneath it all. Small kindnesses for strangers spoke more than any grand gesture ever could.

"Don't mention it," he said, keeping his eyes on their meal.

Lorali scooped dried flowers into a strainer, then reached for the half-full kettle of water she always kept on the stove, hot from his cooking. Her hand pressed against his back to keep her balance as she reached around. The instant her palm made contact, her mind cleared, that throbbing pain gone and chest feeling lighter.

"Holy gods," Eldric gasped.

Lorali blinked, hand hovering over the kettle, the other pressed against him. Clarity was an amazing thing she hadn't realized she'd begun to miss since they parted.

"I think—" she stopped, removing her hand. She groaned as the headache slammed into her with such intensity it sent her hand to his back on instinct; anything to keep it at bay.

"Is that from you?" he asked, hesitantly. She could feel his muscles, still and tense, beneath her palm. As if one movement would bring everything back.

"I think so, let me just see—"

"Lorali don't—"

But her hand was already off him, the pounding pain back, rebounding bright behind her eyes. She felt two strong hands on her arms, pulling her back from the pain that left them both breathless.

"—do that. Don't do that," he finished, eyes boring into her own with such intensity she couldn't look away.

"I'm sorry, I just—" she began to sputter.

"I know," he breathed, fingers flexing gently around her arm. "You're trying to find some kind of control in this situation. I get it, I really do. But your experiments affect me too. Let's try not to play with all the bells and whistles of this bond right at the start. We have time to figure this out."

"Okay," she whispered with a nod. "I'm sorry, I didn't think of it like that."

"It's okay," he said, mouth slanting into a half smile. "This must be why it's called a gallows marriage. We're going to look like an old couple to everyone else."

"Must be." She agreed, peeking around him at the food that was beginning to char. "Your food is burning."

Eldric cursed, twisting to look at the food then back to her.

"Don't let go, I don't want to deal with that again," he said, putting her hand on his side. "Keep a hand on me until we have time to sit down and think."

When she nodded, he turned, her hand running across his abdomen before it settled in the small of his back. With the other, she reached around him to grab the kettle, pouring hot water into the teapot so it could steep. She stood slightly to the side, watching him cook with fascination, turning such simple ingredients into something she could only assume would taste delightful.

"So," he drawled, not looking at her as he flipped the meat in the pan. "Are we going to talk about...?"

"The kiss? Nope," she said with a shake of her head, face heating at the thought of it.

"Got it, got it..." He trailed off, his eyes following the thick god-scrawled lines that connected at her finger.

"I didn't realize we'd be getting matching tattoos." He chuckled, her soft laugh matching his own.

"No, neither did I."

CHAPTER 6

ELDRIC

THEY FINISHED DINNER IN amicable silence, settling on their feet touching beneath the table so they could eat in peace. As he sipped the tea she prepared for him, he couldn't stop his mind from wandering. He loathed that such pain resolved with a simple touch. That his body was no longer his own. That they needed each other—a craving that must be satisfied. He glowered down at the mug, not wanting to look at her.

"You want to talk about it," she said. He could feel her observations from over her own glass and nodded. She hesitated, biting her lip as rose dusted her face, before motioning for him to continue.

He breathed deep, not knowing where to start but setting his cup down anyways. The muscles of her leg tensed beneath his foot, as if she were preparing to run, though he didn't know if either of them would get very far if the pain from earlier was any indication of what was in store for them.

"I don't go around just kissing people," he finally said, voice flat.

"We did what we had to; we shouldn't have to again."

"I don't want to play pretend couple."

"Neither do I."

"How did we even get here." He groaned into his hands. "Thought I'd get married because I wanted to, not because I had to."

Lorali's voice was even, but he saw how her finger fidgeted with the divots and grooves of her mug, the same way she had yesterday when talking about how she thought she had been a distraction. "Do you regret it?"

This piqued his interest, and he thought for a moment before responding.

"No, I don't. I do prefer being alive very much to the alternative."

"If you resent me, it's okay," she said, her voice incredibly small. Not that of the firm woman who had stood before a god just that morning with such confidence. "You didn't choose this; I chose it for you. I understand. I don't blame you."

His brows knit together as he watched her. She didn't sound very okay with the thought at all, as if she were preparing for the worst. A rejection she believed would surely come, but he knew never would. He didn't like it.

Reaching across the table, he brushed his hand against hers, a gentle connection between them. Her grey eyes shot to where their hands met, every muscle tensed as she waited for his next move. She looked as if she really might run, as if she feared his rejection more than anything.

"I don't resent you." He searched her eyes, sincerity dripping from every word. "I'm glad to be alive. You saved me, Lorali Wynmar, and for that I thank you."

He could have sworn he saw silver line her eyes for a moment before she blinked it away, shaking her head with a small smile.

"What a relief. I thought our kiss was so awful that you were having doubts." The joke sounded choked coming from her throat, as if she were fighting back tears. But that spark of fire was back in her eyes. He smirked, taking the bait to play their little game of banter. In general, Eldric hated to see people upset or hurt. But to see the way someone so selfless wore her distress like it was deserved? It settled so poorly within his soul that Eldric knew he'd do anything to prevent her from looking that way ever again.

"Just the opposite. It made me think that whoever gets to marry you for real one day will be a lucky man."

"That's a relief," she chuckled, a blush spreading across her face that let him know all was okay, and he settled back into his seat once more.

"I mean it, Lorali. Thank you."

She nodded at his somber tone.

"Though you don't want to 'play pretend couple,' as you put it, I think we can at least be good partners until our time is up."

He hummed in agreement. It would be best if they got along—they were well and truly stuck with each other now. They may as well get along.

"I think I'd like that." He smiled. "A year is a long time to not become friends with someone like you."

That bright smile snuck across her face before she realized it and she raised her mug toward him. "To friendship, then."

His smile matched her own as he clinked their glasses together.

"To friendship."

***

Curled up on opposite ends of the couch, the pair talked long into the night, learning little bits about each other. Their feet touching, they kept that connection going—both somewhat afraid that the bounding pain would return if they broke contact. He learned that Lorali had a system for everything, and it was best if he didn't touch it. Or else. She learned that prior to their current arrangement, Eldric lived in an old house inherited by his friend. He wouldn't speak further on it and, to his relief, Lorali didn't push.

He watched as she drifted off into slumber, lulled to sleep by the warm fire that was now nothing more than ash and embers. When her breathing slowed and chill crept back into the air, he covered her in one of the countless blankets she had given him to sleep with. Eldric became lost in the crackling fire that died into glowing embers. His mind wandered to the gallows, the previous night, their binding. Seeing Daeson and his sister at their house and explaining it all, learning Daeson had been there with a plan and was just moments away from stopping everything but was too late, unable to beat Lorali's quick wit. Daeson's words clung to him like static long after he returned to Lorali's home. *Playing pretend*—that had been what he'd called it. Though Eldric wasn't thrilled with the arrangement, at this moment he knew that he'd gladly take it over death.

It hadn't hit him, then, how close he'd come to dying. It hadn't hit him until now, sitting in a warm house with a full stomach, a new friend, and a hope for tomorrow. That was something he hadn't experienced in a long while. Tilting his head back, he looked up to the wood beam ceiling and felt silent tears trail into his hair as he realized how truly and utterly thankful he felt to be alive in this moment.

And for the first time in a long time, he prayed. Not to Ostara or even Athanasios or any of their children. But to the high cleric that lay on the other end of the couch sound asleep, unaware of just how completely she had saved him.

Chapter 7

Lorali

ONE THING LORALI HADN'T considered when she claimed her right to a gallows bond, though she hadn't considered anything at all, was the overwhelming stares and watching eyes that would be on her at all times. Especially as she walked with Athera's most wanted at her side. She was used to attention when in her robes or doing official work for the Order, but when the robes were off, she could blend with the crowd. Not anymore. She presumed that's what always happened when one made a public spectacle of themselves—they became the talk of the town. Anyone who had been there that day had seen her face, heard her name, her role in the Order. And word spread like wildfire. Their stares lingering over the thick tattoos inked across the back of her hand that matched Eldric's own. It was a brand for anyone to see, one even her cardigan could not hide. While it was unsettling, she could tolerate it. Would tolerate it. Her companion, on the other hand, looked as if he were about to crawl out of his skin.

"Everyone's staring."

"That's what happens when you're a wanted criminal."

"It's what happens when you're a wanted criminal who gets *caught*. People didn't know my face until two weeks ago." He frowned with arms crossed, matching each and every stare with a glare of his own that turned them away in an instant.

"Shouldn't have gotten caught then," Lorali quipped back on instinct, causing Eldric to nearly choke on his tea.

"Right. On that note, I'll be seeing you." She nodded and turned on her heel. There was little time to think about the lingering eyes—it was her one day off this week and there was shopping to be done, sponsors to be found for the next year's Veridian, and a little treat from her favourite cafe in the upper district with her name on it. Today, she'd take any bit of comfortable solitude she could get.

"Don't be late!" he called after her.

She prepared for the slight tug in her chest. They knew how to fix the pain they were going to face, that there was an end in sight when they finally came back together. It made it dealing with it in the moment easier. She couldn't help but roll her eyes with a smile, adjusting her basket as she kept walking. "I won't."

***

Lorali made her way to the northern edge of the city that housed her favourite bakery. From there, she would head to the market for food and start gauging which businesses were interested in helping with Veridian before enjoying her walk home. She refused to acknowledge the pain that awaited her until she saw Eldric again. It would be a perfectly normal day. She hadn't realized how much she'd craved it until she was finally alone, having pushed through the entire week with little time to stop and just breathe. Some small part of her had wondered if she would ever have a perfectly normal day again. But as she pushed open the bakery door and the smell of fresh baked treats hit her nose, she knew it was a baseless worry. Excitement bounded within her, overjoyed that she could bring such an opportunity to the first shop she had ever spent her hard earned coins at when she moved to Athera.

"Welcome to Emillian's—*Lorali*." Flora's typically cheery voice seemed to freeze in an instant as Lorali let the door shut behind her.

"Hi, Flora." She waved as she stepped up to the counter, the first customer of the day as usual. The young girl's eyes instantly went to the swirling black ink on her hand. Lorali lowered it, tugging her sleeves down at Flora's lingering stare.

"So it's true." Flora's voice was strained. "You did it. I didn't want to believe it, told papa and mama not to believe the rumors, but it's true. You saved that...that *thief*."

Lorali opened her mouth but couldn't object. Could not offer any explanation to the young redhead before her. So, she nodded.

"I did."

Flora swallowed and pressed her lips together, wiping her palms on beautifully embroidered skirts she refused to hide with an apron.

"Papa says you're not welcome here anymore."

Lorali blinked, confused.

"What? I've been buying bread from Emillian for years, before he ever moved to the upper district—"

"And the thief you saved, the thief you married? He's been stealing from us for far longer. Our neighbors too. Papa told me so. He said you knew, and you still saved him."

"Well—yes, but it's more complicated than that—"

"Now you bear the mark of a thief too—you share his sins," she said, looking to where Lorali tried to hide the dark inked scrawl on her skin with a shake of her head.

"That's not true, that's not what this is, this—"

"Papa says you're no longer welcome, Lorali." The young girl's face was sad as she glanced behind her to the kitchen. "You should go before he realizes you're here. He's not very happy."

Lorali was at a loss for words, looking between the girl and the kitchen behind her with a sinking feeling that this might not be the first time she encountered this today.

"O-Okay," she breathed, nodding as she released her fists to keep calm. "Tell Emillian that I'm sorry. That if he wants to talk about it, he knows where to find me." Lorali did her best to smile as she placed a small coin on the counter before turning to go. "As a thank you for all these years. May Ostara's light shine upon you."

"We don't need your blessings or your coin," Flora said, pushing the coin back her way. "Goodbye, Lorali."

She did not take the coin back, making her way out the door and back onto familiar streets that had never seemed so daunting. With tight shoulders and measured breaths, she prepared to go about her day that she now knew with certainty would be anything but normal.

CHAPTER 8

ELDRIC

"SHE'S STILL NOT TALKING to me," Eldric said, watching as Kaela immediately turned around and stayed outside when she spotted him through the kitchen window. Daeson shook his head. The old summer home was alive, buzzing with people who were part of their cause and helped with the distribution of resources among the less fortunate in Athera. Many of them were children when they came here, but were now growing taller, their voices deepening. Becoming men and women before his very eyes. Learning to give back in the same way they had been helped.

"You almost died. You're like another brother to her. She's just processing."

Eldric winced. "Shouldn't she be happy I'm alive, then?"

"You know my sister," Daeson said with a shrug.

"I know Kaela," he sighed, resigned.

"She'll talk when she's ready; don't push it." Daeson clapped him on the shoulder before heading into the basement as if he spoke from experience. Eldric followed, running a hand through his hair.

His chest pulled toward the city where Lorali was running her errands. He had gone far enough; the pounding ache started as he neared the countryside home settled just outside the city. It'd become a constant companion over these past two weeks, the dull tug that became a sharp pain when he crossed the estate's bridge. Telling him to turn back, that he had gone too far. Just as it had on the day of their binding.

"How's married life? The wife? Any thoughts of children yet?" his friend's voice teased as he descended the stairs, and Eldric couldn't help but scowl.

"It's not like that between us, Daeson. I told you. We live our lives separately and come together as required by the bond. That's it."

"You've moved in with her."

"Because I had to."

Daeson rounded the last step, lighting a candle on the wall with the stroke of a match and using it to illuminate the room filled with papers atop a crowded table. The flickering flame reflected in the old lucernas embedded into the wall that hadn't functioned in years.

"Right, right...." he trailed off, rifling through papers as he looked for something specific. "Have you slept with her yet?"

Eldric nearly tripped at that as he came off the stairs, catching himself on a support beam that creaked more than either of them would have liked. He winced, removing his hands slowly, knowing it was ridiculous but worried he could bring the whole house toppling down.

"Have I—gods, *no*. She's not just any member of the Order, Daeson, she's a *high cleric*."

It would be unthinkable. While Lorali was kind and welcoming, Eldric didn't forget where her loyalties lay. Couldn't forget. Before today, he had only ever seen her in the Order's robes to the point he'd wondered if she owned any other clothes. It took everything within him to remember that she was not the rest of the Order's members. Her actions so far had proven her selfless and brave. So different from what he had seen his first time on the Order's doorstep. But still, she served them just as he served the city.

He initially had his doubts about her desire for friendship, but decided to make their situation amicable at least. He didn't know if he could spend the rest of the year in such constant pain. It was distracting, fogging his mind more as the distance between them grew. How she continued her work in the temple, so focused that she came back to the cottage late in the evening and left before the sun rose, was beyond him. He didn't think she slept—coming home with texts or parchments to read as she searched for any information related to gallows bonds. He hadn't gathered the courage to ask her why she stayed up hours into the night with her nose in a book, fearful of what the answer would be. Darkness had set in beneath her lashes, but her eyes were alight with study.

"I know you're a romantic at heart. Waiting to woo her before consummating your marriage, I see." Daeson's teasing chuckle died on his lips as he patted Eldric's cheek. He paused, brows knitted together, mind turning as it worked through something that brought confusion to his dark eyes.

"Why was there a high cleric at the gallows? That's work usually reserved for acolytes."

"I don't know," Eldric said with a shake of his head. There wasn't enough information for him to speculate. He'd rather not talk about Lorali here; it made his chest tighten, like she would somehow know through the bond where he was. As if he were betraying his vow to her just by being in his friend's presence.

He braced his hands on the table, looking down and staring at hastily drawn diagrams scratched onto parchment in smeared ink and scrambled letters with Daeson's small handwriting just beneath them spelling out the once encrypted words. Puzzled, he stared at them, trying to place the familiar glass dome until realization dawned. The skylight dome was familiar because he had been beneath it just a few weeks ago. His eyes followed the arrows that showed a hidden panel, hinges blended perfectly in the soldered seams. A maintenance hatch. Scrawled runes that showed how someone could bypass the protective wards placed around the top of the building.

"Where'd you get this?" he breathed in disbelief, ghosting his fingers across the fine parchment and lifting it to find more underneath, the code only half deciphered. He stared down at the plans and papers littering the table, quietly scanning the document that rested on top that his friend had already translated. Whoever Daeson's source was, they had to be someone of high standing.

"A new informant." Daeson raised a brow, a smug grin spreading across his features the way it always did when he was scheming. As if lightning were about to strike. "I'm thinking it's time the Order of Ostara returned what belongs to the Atheras."

Eldric watched the shadows dance across Daeson's dark skin in the flickering lowlight, mixing with his inky hair. The same hair that would have borne the stolen silver and moonstone circlet meant for the ruler of Athera. Sometimes he forgot Daeson's lineage—that the man he stood beside was a lost prince, meant to rule over the Valley of Wind. That if Korinth's Order of the Star hadn't toppled the six kingdoms of Euphedos centuries ago, he would have been king. Then there were moments like this, where an undercurrent of power rippled just beneath his skin, setting his hair on edge, and Eldric couldn't help but remember that the slight point to Daeson's ears was a warning. Marked him as something more powerful than a mere human could ever hope to be.

Turning away, Eldric dragged his hands across his face, a strangled noise caught in his throat. Taking back the lost crown was something that they'd joked about after Daeson convinced Eldric of his identity. A dream between scorned boys who grew into cunning men and finally realized they weren't invincible. Their approach had to be clever—just as clever as the ones they were fighting.

"Why now—what changed? I thought we put this idea to rest years ago."

His friend's palms rested on the table across from him, eyes bright and smile wild. "You. That's what changed. With that cleric, you've become our person on the inside. They plan to keep you close—and that will be their downfall. Sylvene is smiling brightly upon us; we must take advantage of this fortune."

Eldric was quiet, stomach sinking as he saw Daeson's plan coming together in his mind. To take advantage of the situation. Of Lorali's goodwill and trust she'd placed in him. With her as a stepping stone, he'd elevate himself to greater heights, fueled by his dedication to the greater good. The thought of warm tea by the fire turned sour at the memory of promises sworn years ago beneath a blade.

Oathbreaker.

That word shattered through him, pulsing with the ache of their bond.

Which oath did he keep—one he had sworn long ago to the person who had helped him when he was at his lowest? Or the one he made before the gods, inked into his very soul?

"If I—"

"If?" His friend balked, thrown off-kilter by just two words. "I thought we were a team."

"I want to help, Daeson, I do—but this bond between me and the cleric is more than just words. I am branded. Tied to her in ways I—I don't even know how to explain. If I'm caught, it's not just me condemned to the gallows."

"All the more reason they'd never suspect you. You are the only one who can do this," Daeson said, eyes leveling with him. His jaw set firm as he stepped to Eldric and they stood eye to eye. "Are your loyalties with me? Or with her?"

Eldric remained quiet, frustration shaking within his very bones.

"Or do you still harbor loyalty to the guard?"

"Stop it!" Eldric growled, hand hitting the table. His heart raged and his breathing grew ragged. Daeson stoked the embers of hatred that rested within Eldric's heart with practiced precision the way only one who knew the other's soul could. The pair stood, assessing each other in flickering silence. His whispering voice cracked as he regained control and spoke again. "I am loyal to Athera—and *you* are Athera. The rightful heir. I am loyal to you. But I can't put someone innocent at risk."

"She is a cleric within the Order—she is far from innocent."

"You don't know that," Eldric whispered as he shook his head. "It's only been a few weeks, but I think she's different."

"Does she use her magic to aid those who are unable to pay the Order's tithes? Or help feed the hungry from her own pocket?" Daeson asked, anger simmering within as he moved around the table. "That archcleric and their Order took a thriving kingdom and reduced its leaders to puppet figureheads that agree with anything for the right price, leaving the people struggling to survive. Starving to the point we have to take it into our own hands. And they almost killed you for it. I don't know what I would have done if you had died." Daeson's voice broke at that, hand brushing up Eldric's arm before squeezing his shoulder. There were years of knowing in that touch, of trust and triumphs, of heartbreaks and failures endured together.

"I can't do this without you. Why else would the goddess have sent that cleric to grant you a second chance at life if not to make a difference? It's finally time to return this kingdom to its former glory. Make it into something better. Something fair. What we've been working towards."

Daeson's face softened, lips pressed together as Eldric couldn't help but bend.

He glanced to the shadowed corners, finding that they reminded him too much of Athanasios' swirling landscape, knowing that it hadn't been the wind goddess or even Ostara who had granted him a second chance at life.

CHAPTER 9

LORALI

ORALI KNEW ELDRIC MEANT well, wanting to share in the work to keep the household, but she couldn't have him with her when she went shopping. Most of the stores she had frequented for years no longer allowed her business—Emillian, the butcher, the farmer who supplied her grain and eggs. They all made it clear she was no longer welcome. She doubted they would even listen if she were to speak to them regarding official business, leaving her at a loss for where to go next.

The passing of the last frost brought a sense of relief and gratitude to her heart. She made an offering to Ostara as her garden flourished with an abundance of early spring vegetables that would keep them fed. She kept the reason for the recent scarcity of their food supply to herself, unable to share it with Eldric, who remained blissfully unaware. He was a resourceful and frugal cook, using every scrap and piece of stale bread at their disposal for some sort of meal. Delighted with the assortment of herbs she had stored, he'd made sure every meal was bursting with flavor no matter the contents.

"The weather's good today, Lor—you won't even need those gloves. What kind of housemate would I be if I didn't at least help carry the heavy stuff?" His smile was a gentle breeze that could keep her grey clouds at bay, but only for a moment. "You've been busy with work; I've hardly seen you. Plus, I'd rather not deal with any...*side effects* of the bond."

She tried to return that smile, but it didn't reach her eyes as she tugged her sleeves down, making sure every bit of their matching mark was covered. "We're only low on rice, I'll grab a bag and be back. It's not worth the trip for both of us."

She ignored how his brows knit together, arms crossed in a near pout as she grabbed the woven basket from beside the door and made to leave. He cursed softly as her hand took the doorknob and she paused.

"You don't even need those gloves," he whispered, as if it were a realization. "How could I be so stupid? Of course I can't go to the market with you. It's because of me, isn't it? Our bond."

Lorali turned to face him, pressing her back against the door. She couldn't look at him as he walked toward her.

"I don't want to lie to you, Eldric—"

"Then don't." He stood steps away, glancing down at her gloved hand. "Tell me. You don't have to protect me from them; I stopped caring what others thought of me long ago."

Lip between her teeth, Lorali weighed her words carefully.

"It's not what they think of you, it's what they think of me. Many of the usual sellers I've gone to for years are refusing my business, so I'm having to find new ones. It should be easier now that spring is here—we'll grow some vegetables to help substitute. Take any of the extras and preserve them for the winter. It'll be easier now that it's not just me alone doing the work—"

She babbled, filling the silence as the knot in his throat bobbed. He stared at her, processing what she said. Putting pieces into place before he finally cut her off, expression unreadable save for his tight jaw and disbelieving voice.

"By the light, Lorali, that's been six weeks—"

"I know, I know." She waved her hand as if to clear the air between them. "It's fine, really. I didn't want to tell you because I knew you'd do that."

"Do what?"

"Beat yourself up for it like I'm not the one who dragged us into this."

"I'm not—I wasn't—" Eldric sputtered but couldn't deny the accusation. "For the record, I don't think it was you who dragged us into this, but Athanasios. Think the sick bastard got off on watching us get married then shoving us off—"

"Do not speak ill of him in my house!" Lorali sounded like a tea kettle as she jumped forward and clamped her hands over his mouth. "He is a *god*. He can *hear you*, and made sure we knew so the last time we saw him."

Looking down at her, Eldric nodded with wide eyes as she continued.

"It is fine. If they want to lose my business based on my own decisions and their refusal to listen, let them. It's their loss. I don't need you to call the ire of the *very generous god* who gave you a second chance at life down upon my house. So apologize and leave an offering on the altar. He likes the honeyed whiskey I keep on the third shelf. Got it?"

Eldric gave a muffled agreement. She removed her hands from his lips as he whispered an apology—to her or Athanasios, she didn't know. All she did know was that as she left, he was reaching for the bottle on the shelf like she'd told him to, and she couldn't help but smile.

***

A fresh bowl of starberries and a muddled drink was the last thing Lorali expected to come home to. She wasn't complaining.

"What's this?"

"A thank you, and an apology." Eldric offered her the glass as she set the sack of rice she'd hauled home on the counter. "By far, my life has improved in the last six weeks. I hadn't thought about how our arrangement might have affected your life. So it's a thank you for your generosity and a sorry for not realizing sooner."

She couldn't help but smile as she clinked her drink to his, their toast from weeks prior unspoken in her mind. *To friendship.*

"Unnecessary," she started, taking a sip of the delicious drink and humming her delight despite the slight tangy flavor of a few unripe berries that must have slipped in. "But much appreciated. I'm just happy to have someone else cook for a change."

"While I'm under your roof, you won't have to cook a thing. Mostly because I don't want to subject myself to whatever it is you call cooking again. A little less altruistic and a little more self preservation. But the results are the same."

"Right, right." She couldn't help but roll her eyes, following him out the door and down the stone path through the garden. "What I'm really curious about is where you found these starberries. Last I recall, I wasn't growing any."

Fresh green sprouts erupted from the dark plots of soil, rising to meet the sun. The rough oval leaves of her sage shrub were flourishing, breaking away with ease in her hand from the woody stem. That crisp and earthy smell was bright between her fingers, bringing a smile to her face as she plopped the herb into her drink.

"You learn where to forage when the seasons permit. These are picked fresh from one of my favourite spots near the city, just for you. This patch is rather small—it doesn't produce as much as I'd like, but it gets the job done. But I was spoiled with one of the best starberry patches in Euphedos growing up in the mountains." He grinned.

She took one of the tangy sweet berries from the bowl, biting into its yellow skin, giving way to blue flesh as she finished it in two bites, tossing the last bit attached to the leafy green top toward her compost.

"I'd love it if you showed me some time—I haven't done much exploring outside the city. Ever, really."

Her eyes lit with joy when she noticed the cheese platter waiting for her on the garden table. She shuddered to think what she'd do if Charline had turned her away like the others—that woman made the best cheese in all of Athera and Lorali doubted she could settle for anything else now.

Fruit, drinks, cheese—this truly was an apology; an unneeded one, but thorough. While having to find new vendors to work with was a pain to be sure, she couldn't resent Eldric for it. He was thoughtful, kind, a little too hard on himself thinking he had to carry the world on his shoulders. She hoped that maybe during their year, she could show him that it was okay to lean on people. That the Order had the best interests of the people at heart, and that rather than stepping outside the law to make a difference, he could work within it.

"Surely, you have at some point. Explored any neighboring villages? Gone for an evening stroll?"

Lorali shook her head and Eldric looked dumbstruck.

"You've never been outside the city? Not once?"

She shrugged, looking out over her small garden and wondering what else outside of this she could possibly need.

"I was nine when I was brought to Athera and taken in by the Order. Lived in the temple for most of that time. During instruction, you aren't able to leave until it's complete and after I was done I... just haven't thought about it."

"Nine?" His voice was light, but his brows creased as his mind did the math. "That means you've been part of the Order for..."

"Eighteen years." She nodded.

"What happened to your parents?" There was something in his voice, catching on itself as he asked. As if he knew that for someone so young to be left to the Order, there was only one reason. She shifted in her seat, throat feeling tight and heartbeat picking up. Even after all these years, foggy memories and unpleasant feelings still surfaced, clinging to her like spiderwebs. Not letting her go.

"We were moving to Athera when our cart was attacked outside the city walls. They...didn't make it." Her answer was rehearsed, stiff, but it was all she could do to keep herself distanced from those memories that had plagued her as nightmares for far too long. Pressing her lips into a thin line, she didn't give him time to respond. Time to process what she'd revealed. She didn't want his pity or his condolences. It was an awful thing that happened to her, but she'd moved past it.

"What about you? I imagine one doesn't turn to your line of work due to anything pleasant."

Her words came out more abrasive than she intended, but Eldric took it in stride. He blew out a breath, meeting her eyes with a gentle look.

"I guess we're not talking about that then?"

"No, we're not."

He nodded, solemn as he tipped his drink back and downed half of it in one go. "My mother was an entertainer. We lived a happy but simple life together until she passed when I was fourteen. I felt the status quo was unjust and found others who felt the same, so we decided to do something about it."

Lorali eyed him over her glass as she sipped the blue concoction, getting a pleasant surprise of unmuddled starfruit as her drink neared the bottom. She could tell there was more there, and wondered if it had to do with Fulke calling him an oathbreaker. She wouldn't pry, just as he didn't. They would tell each other their stories in their own time.

"An entertainer? What kind?"

He nodded, a soft smile crossing his face as he remembered. Magic sparked to life as he waved his fingertips before him, leaving traces of firelight dancing in the air between them.

"She danced, using her magic to create spectacular shows that would draw crowds. I inherited a bit, but it's party tricks compared to hers." Those sparks whirled and whizzed around them, Eldric controlling them with the tip of his finger. Where he pointed, they followed. As his chuckle turned into a sigh, his gaze turned wistful. "She was a great mother. We didn't have much, but we had enough."

Lorali watched the glimmer of magic fade, his magic so different from her own. She wondered if she had ever seen his mother dance at any of the Veridian festivals before she passed. Wondered what it'd be like to use her own magic outside of communing with the gods. She'd never gotten the chance, those first specks of true potential only showing after the Order took her in. The thought of using magic for herself rather than others felt foreign and wrong, but she thought about what that freedom to express herself would be like and thought that maybe, one day, she may be brave enough to try.

CHAPTER 10

ELDRIC

THE RAINY SPRING ENDED and brought about a summer heat that scorched the air and scalded the skin with no relief. Heated haze clung to the ground, refusing to let go. As if it were waiting for the summer solstice just days away before it would consider releasing its grip.

He'd been sure the shimmering heat played tricks with his vision when he saw a familiar figure crouched in the distance beneath a tree. He was all too familiar with the lithe build, recognizing it in an instant once he realized it was no trick of the light. Daeson was on the side of the road, cradling someone in his arms beneath a shady tree.

The girl's short brown curls clung to her pale yet ruddy face in sweat-soaked strands and her parched lips parted, wanting water yet unable to lift it to her mouth. Daeson took the canteen of water and trickled it into her mouth, slowly. Making sure she swallowed every drop before he gave her more to keep her from choking,

He looked up, face guarded until he realized who had found him and the mask dissolved into relief tinged with an edge of panic.

"Thank the wind it's you." He gave a weary chuckle. "I found her like this—I don't know how long it's been. Do you think it's heat sickness?"

"It could be," Eldric murmured, pressing his fingers to the pulse point just below her jaw. It was weak and thready, beating fast as a hummingbird's wings. "Though I don't think I've seen it quite this bad before. Quick, help me get these layers off her."

"She needs a healer. I think—" Eldric started, moving his focus to loosening the girl's clothes. Sweat poured in buckets down the girl's back, soaking through the smock that stuck against her skin and dampening the strings of her kirtle. She slumped against him as Daeson shifted, pulling the many layers off her and leaving only the thin garment clinging to her skin. He put an arm around her to help keep her upright. "I think we should take her to Lorali; she'll know what to do."

Daeson's clothes were drenched with sweat, as if he had run miles before he came upon her. "No, all we need to do is get her out of this heat. She'll improve once she's somewhere cool. Help me get her to the house."

"Why don't you take her and I can go get Lorali—"

"*No.* We will get the girl out of the heat, and she will be fine." Daeson's voice rose, cutting him off. Stubborn as always. "We do not need her. We're not involving people we can't trust unless necessary."

Eldric held his stare for a long moment; breathing had become difficult in the oppressive humid air. His eyes trailed the way he had come. The road that led back to Lorali's. She was a cleric, she healed people for a living. But Daeson was right, it was too far; the old summer home Daeson had inherited was just over the bridge and around the bend. Besides, he didn't want Lorali involved in or anywhere near his personal life. It was too risky. Maybe Daeson was right—the girl would improve just by being somewhere cool. The old wards on the Athera house still had traces of wind magic that kept it chilly even on the hottest days. It could work.

"It'll take longer for me to get there while I'm carrying her. Go ahead of me, get supplies. Clear the living room. Have everything ready when I get there." Eldric gave instructions as he pulled his shirt over his head in one quick motion, using it to wipe as much sweat from the girl's body as possible before they were on the move. Daeson's eyes lingered for a moment, hesitant, before he nodded and ran to prepare his home for their unplanned guest.

When she was as dry as he could get her, Eldric scooped her into his arms, cradling her against his chest. She was so small; she couldn't be more than sixteen. What could she have possibly been doing all the way out here alone? The girl gave a small gasp, and when he looked down he saw her eyelids flutter open for just a moment.

"*Hey*—hey there, it's okay. I've got you. We're taking you somewhere to cool down," he said in a soft, gentle voice. Trying to do his best to exude a calmness that could soothe any nerves or any worries, the way Lorali did. "What's your name?"

Her eyes couldn't focus as she gazed up at him, her form slumping against him as if keeping her eyes open took all the strength her body had. Her lips moved, forming a word he couldn't make out. She tried again, voice weak and cracking, but louder this time.

"Saraina."

"*Saraina*," he said. He could feel the old sweat of her underdress seeping against his skin. "We're going to keep you safe. I promise."

She fell unconscious again, and he covered her head and torso with his shirt, hoping to keep as much of the sun off her as possible. His stomach was in knots as he ran with the girl in his arms, ignoring the pounding ache that worsened as he crossed the bridge, that tether telling him he was once again going too far. He fought through it until the manor's stairs were in sight, door open and Daeson's sister, Kaela, standing in the doorway.

She met him just off the stairs, leading him to the living room where several of the other girls waited. Eldric laid her down on the makeshift pallet bed on the floor.

"You should—"

"Go somewhere else for a minute," Kaela stopped him. "We've got this."

"Go somewhere—what?" he sputtered as Kaela crowded into his space, pushing him back. The fabric of a fresh underdress in Kaela's hand brushed his skin. One of the girls removed his shirt and he realized that her garment was practically see-through with sweat; he paled at the nauseating thought of others looking at her in such a vulnerable state. Shame rose within him—he'd never considered that until now. He'd been so focused on just getting her here, saving her, that the thought hadn't even crossed his mind.

"Understood," he said with a curt nod, turning away and heading to the kitchen to try and do something to help.

After an hour of changing cooling rags on a near constant basis and fanning Saraina as best they could, she was no longer sweating, her skin turning dry and hot. That once thready pulse now bounded beneath her skin. Bright red seeped into her skin and soon, she couldn't take even a sip of water, only able to turn her head to the side and vomit. It made his skin crawl and stomach knot with unease. Something didn't feel right.

They stood at a distance, watching as their friends, their comrades, worked hard to keep Saraina comfortable. Eldric paced, while Daeson stood statue still with arms crossed. Eldric knew he felt it too—things weren't improving. She was, somehow, getting worse.

"She needs a healer," Eldric murmured. Daeson's jaw was tight, eyes focused on the work being done before them.

"Do you trust her?" he asked, refusing to look at Eldric.

Eldric stopped, thinking—truly thinking. Did he trust her enough to risk everything, to risk Daeson? Would she run and tell the guard where they were hiding, or tell the Order that the lost son of Athera was hidden just outside their walls?

I have to believe that someone who would steal from nobles to care for the people of this city would be a man of honor.

Those words had shocked him, revealing more than she knew. The trust she placed in him to not abandon her to the consequences. That they, fundamentally, held the same beliefs. She knew the city suffered and did what she could to help. He did the same—just in a different way.

He swallowed, glancing to Daeson, who finally met his eyes.

"I do."

Daeson's face looked pained, but he nodded. "Then go get her."

***

He sprinted down the street that had grown familiar in the last several months, the tall trees providing much-needed shade with their long shadows as he neared the last house. Eldric could see their small garden, overflowing with lush summer crops that peeked out of their beds. The sunflowers he'd planted reached towards the sky—a bright beacon for him to follow home. He shouted her name, knowing she'd be there.

"El?" she called, voice laced with concern. She must have heard his feet hitting the dirt and pebble path as he rounded the corner. "El, what's wrong?"

"I need your help," was all he said, chest heaving as their eyes met. And without word or question, Lorali dropped her tools, ripped off her gardening gloves, and ran to him. Staying at his side all the way back to the Athera house.

***

That sharp mind of hers needed no direction when she entered the house, pausing for only a moment to assess the situation. Recognition sparked in her eyes when she saw the girl on the floor.

"She's still unconscious. I don't know if any of this is working," Kaela said, a hint of panic edging her voice, thick with unshed tears. Lorali rushed forward, stepping through the group, and taking a place at her side.

Knowing what to do in an instant, she pressed fingers against Saraina's pulse point, pulled back her eyelids, placed her ear to the girl's chest and listened.

"You did good keeping her stable until I got here." Lorali inclined her head towards Kaela, dismissing everyone else who scrambled off in a hurry. "You, stay here—everyone else, go."

"Why isn't she getting better? Last summer when Jira had heat sickness, just getting him out of the sun was enough."

"It's progressing—she's completely overheated and there are other factors at play. But it's okay. I'm going to help her," Lorali said, giving Kaela's hand a small squeeze.

"Was there anyone with her? Where was her father? A guard?" she asked, not turning to look at him as she set to work taking a stray piece of burnt wood from the fire and drawing marks onto the floor that surrounded Saraina. He could only make out the shape of a star, a wave, and a scrawling wind, each encircled in a runic language he did not know. One meant only for the gods and those that served them.

"No one. She was by herself, beneath a tree. I found her. That's it." Daeson tensed, on edge.

"Okay, okay," she breathed, hands hovering as her eyes flickered over Saraina's body, murmuring to herself as if she were running through a list to make sure she had everything she would need. She had that same determined crease to her brow as she did during their bonding ceremony. It made his breath catch. He couldn't help the fond feeling that overcame him. She was in her element, all confidence and knowledge. It was something he found he rather enjoyed seeing.

"Heat sickness can turn from uncomfortable to fatal in a heartbeat," she said, breathing steadily as she took two rags dripping with water from the bucket. He watched as she placed one rag over Saraina's chest and the other over her navel, the dripping water darkening her thin summer dress. "It's a good thing Eldric brought me. Any later and she'd have died."

An eerie stillness settled over the room; not even the house stirred in the familiar presence of an oncoming storm. Her palms hovered above Saraina's heart and naval as she whispered words he couldn't understand. He could pick out pieces, familiar names of deities.

Ostara, mother of light.

Aesis, guardian of the waters.

Sylvene, guardian of the winds.

A shivering breeze brushed through the house, causing his hair to stand on edge. Eldric hadn't seen her magic since they were bound before Athanasios. She hadn't used writing then, but she hadn't been asking for help—just an audience. The markings on the floor flared to life, matching the soft and gentle glow emitting from her palms as he realized they were instructions. A way to command the power of gods.

Lorali's eyes were not her own—bright and unseeing, yet missing nothing. The eyes of a goddess. He swallowed, still as his eyes met hers. He didn't dare look away first. Water glowed beneath her palms, the cleric's hands moving in slow, purposeful motions. As if they were being guided across Saraina's body. Light flared to life within the room, bursting from Lorali as if she were the sun itself.

Heartbeats passed before it dimmed and they could see again, watching as Saraina's breathing eased, no longer the shallow and ragged saw of her chest it had been. Her skin calmed, no longer a bright and worrisome red as it settled into a natural, healthy olive tone.

The room was stunned into silence. How was it possible for a person to channel the guidance of the gods without being burned alive? Not just *a* god, *multiple* gods. All working in tandem, helping her achieve her goal. This was power in its rawest form. Sure, strong, fine-tuned, and used with ease as she worked ceaselessly to help a stranger without question. The woman once chosen to be the next archcleric—the change they needed.

It left him in awe, heart aching with sudden, crashing realization. A whisper dark and cold passed through Eldric, as if Athanasios himself heard his heart and agreed. As if it were the sole reason he had been saved.

The woman before him, selfless and unafraid, was everything he wanted. Everything he wished he could be and more. He had never been a man of faith, but to him she was divine, and he would spend the rest of his life worshiping and believing in only her. It was sacrilege and salvation all at once. A chosen poison and cure—both of which he would gladly take again and again. She was the only one who mattered in this unforgiving world, and he knew he'd be a fool to ever let her go.

Saraina's eyes fluttered open for a brief moment, glancing side to side as she took in the faces of strangers peering over her. Kaela pushed short brown curls back from her forehead and smiled down.

"Hey, it's okay," Kaela whispered sweetly, giving her shoulder a light squeeze. The girl gave a weak nod, giving a sigh of relief as she fell into a restful sleep.

Eldric looked over at Lorali, that glowing light and far away look fading from her eyes. He could tell the moment she was herself once more, not missing the way she wobbled the slightest bit as she came out of the trance. Her hands pressed against the ground to stay steady, a thin sheen of sweat across her brow. He wanted to rush to her side, to take her hand and not let go. She had performed a miracle—but instead of taking pride in her work, Lorali's expression tipped downward into a frown as she looked at the now sleeping girl.

"Saraina, what were you *thinking*?" she whispered with a shake of her head.

Eldric felt Daeson still beside him, not looking over as he whispered. "Did you tell her the girl's name?"

Brows furrowed, thinking, Eldric shook his head. "No—I told her the situation, but I don't think I mentioned a name...why?"

Daeson was quiet for a moment before stepping to Eldric, leaning with a slight glance. "Neither has anyone else in the room. So how does she know it?"

They both turned, looking back at Lorali who was fussing with the girl. "Why did she ask about her father or guard, like she knew this girl should have had one? Seem to know that Saraina had something wrong with her, making things worse?"

"Stop it—you're not doing this again. Taking someone's kindness and warping it to fit your idea of the world. I'm sure there's a logical explanation."

"For a girl to show up nearly dead on my running path outside my property in the woods? For the cleric you're bound to knowing her? This smells like a trap and you're too much a fool, falling for her tricks, to see it."

"*Not everyone is out to get you.*" The moment the words left his mouth, Eldric wished he could take them back. Swallow them whole as Daeson went stone still.

"Say that to my ancestors," he hissed, knocking Eldric's shoulder as he stormed from the room.

CHAPTER 11

LORALI

"Saraina, by Ostara's light, what were you thinking?" Lorali murmured with her head in her hands. She was finally alone, sitting on the floor with silent tears slipping through her lashes as she thought of losing the girl she knew to be so kind and caring and unafraid. Her heart ached, the thought of what would have happened if she was too late pulling a whimper from her throat.

At the sound of footsteps approaching, Lorali wiped away her tears, composing herself. Familiar brown leather boots stopped before her. Lorali's gaze trailed up to find Eldric's suntanned face staring back at her, his hair wild from worried hands running through it.

"Can I?" he asked, gesturing to the spot beside her on the floor. She gave a nod, scooting slightly so he could lean against the couch with her. They stayed like that, blessedly quiet, as she looked at Saraina, just waiting for her to wake up. Eldric fidgeted at her side, his fingers interlocked and thumb running across his palm in that way he did when there was something he wanted to say but didn't know how. She didn't have it in her to pry it out of him and settled into the silence while he searched for what to say.

"So, you know her? Saraina?" he finally asked. She raised a brow, unable to believe that was the question that had him so worked up. She nodded.

"I've been treating her monthly for the last three years at the temple. She's become like a younger sister of sorts." Lorali chuckled, shaking her head as she gazed down at Saraina lovingly. She still remembered that first meeting when Archcleric Sage had introduced her to councilman Stellian Dumont, desperate for a cure to his daughter's illness. As he was a generous donator to the Order, Sage felt called to help. Looking back now, Lorali could see how the archcleric had begun to weave responsibility into her daily duties, testing her to see if she could take their place.

Lorali's healing capabilities are second only to mine, Sage had said with a squeeze of her shoulder. *I wish I could help you personally, but she comes with my recommendation and my blessing. I have no doubt she will help your daughter immensely.*

Councilman Dumont would do anything to keep Saraina healthy and safe until he found a cure. He told her everything—how it had started with a rash six months ago that spread across the bridge of her nose. They tried many ointments and salves from the local healers, but none of them helped. But then Saraina became weak and fatigued, her joints aching as if she were not sixteen, but sixty, making it difficult for her to even move. He called her frail, incapable of even holding a cup. And Lorali had believed him—until she met Saraina for herself. Even at the tender age of thirteen, Saraina's stubborn streak was apparent. Lorali knew the girl's father would never understand and that she was twice as clever as any guard he would ever assign to watch her. She was sick, not dying. There was a life to be lived, and Lorali knew the girl wouldn't just let it pass her by.

"Her body's sensitive to the heat, so the summers are usually hardest on her. To be out alone on a day like today, she must have been up to no good." Lorali's chuckle was empty, no humor behind it. Tiredness had seeped so deep into her bones, she didn't know if it would ever leave.

She noticed that Eldric was staring at her, slack-jawed. Her nose wrinkled, feeling exposed beneath his gaze.

"What?"

"You do that—" he gestured to Saraina and the markings surrounding her "—every *month?*"

"Not quite. This time was... different." Lorali closed her eyes, taking a shuddering breath. Her voice only came out in a whisper as she continued, head cradled in her hands.

"Ostara spoke to me when I entered the room and saw Saraina lying there. I had this feeling within me, within my gut, that I would need more. She was so close to death. I didn't know if I would pull her back. Didn't think I could. But then I knew I must call upon Aesis and Sylvene, to enlist their aid. And Ostara guided me, showed me how to incorporate them into her healing ritual I already knew. It was—"

Hot tears spilled over her cheeks in waves. She wanted to forget it happened. Didn't want to think about the way it felt to have the energy of three gods tangle within her body, touch her very soul. Within the Order, the other gods were honored and respected. They never took power from another deity. It went against every teaching. She didn't know what it meant if Ostara herself had guided her to do so. Didn't know what others at the Order would think when they learned of it.

"—amazing," Eldric finished for her, taking her hands from where she hid her face and holding them tight. "It was amazing, Lorali. You were amazing. You saved her life."

His smile was sweet and warm, like the hands that now held hers. Though her face was warm and wet with tears, she couldn't help but smile. At least there was one person who thought so. She noticed that the shadows had grown long, the sun finally beginning to rest and put away its oppressive midday heat until tomorrow, while the valley breeze swept in.

"Thank you," she whispered, squeezing his hands back. "I think it's time we head back to town; we need to get her home."

She nodded toward Saraina, who breathed softly as her body recuperated. Eldric nodded, standing. "Let me tell the others, then we'll go."

Lorali nodded in agreement, eyes following him as he left and taking in the room for the first time. It would have once been nice, quaint even. But the ornate wallpaper was faded, furniture within it old and worn and in desperate need of repair. She stood to stretch her legs as she looked at one of the many dusty portraits of a young, happy family on the mantel that hadn't been moved in ages—all with matching dark hair and pointed ears, reminding her of the old paintings of forgotten kings that collected dust in the temple's basement. She wondered who they were, the original owners of the home. What could have happened to them for Eldric and his friends to end up living here, leaving the dark hardwood floors covered in scuffs and scrapes accumulated over years of boots trodding across them. She took in the dazzling chandelier in the center of the room she hadn't noticed earlier, brushing her hand carefully along the wall moulding as she continued her curious explorations.

"*—I don't care, I don't trust her,*" a voice said in an agitated whisper from the other room across from the foyer. Lorali froze when she heard Eldric's voice in response.

"Daeson, I told you there was a logical explanation and there is."

"Right, it conveniently happens to be the person she takes care of. Seems like a load of shit to me. Have you ever thought that she could be lying to you?"

Lorali held her breath, waiting as the silence dragged on to the point where she wanted to beg him to answer.

"Yes, I have," he finally said with a sigh. She could see him in her mind's eye, running his hand through his hair in that frustrated way he did. She couldn't help but feel a twinge of pain within her heart at the admission. The other man not trusting her, she understood. She was a stranger. But for Eldric to think she could be lying after all these months? She shouldn't hold it against him; it was a statement she wasn't meant to hear. But it still hurt.

"Then why can't you see what's right in front of you?" the other man—Daeson—asked, his voice calm but steadily rising. She recognized it, then. He was the one who originally found Saraina.

"Because I don't think she is," Eldric hissed, his feet moving farther away from the door. "You don't know her, I do. So you don't have to trust her, you have to trust me. Trust that I know her well enough to know she isn't lying. Are you really going to jeopardize—"

His voice dropped so low she could barely hear it over the thrum of her own heart. Lorali stepped forward to try and listen more, but the creak of an old floorboard beneath her foot made both men pause. She could only hear their breaths as she straightened up, deciding the time for snooping was done as she called out.

"Eldric? Everything okay in there? I don't want it to get too late; we still need to take Saraina home."

She stepped a couple of paces, feigning innocence as she rounded the corner. They were standing nose to nose, Eldric's finger pressed into Daeson's chest. Their stares stayed locked on the other, until Eldric finally looked away first.

"Sorry to interrupt, I'll just—"

"No, it's fine. I was just telling Daeson we're leaving," Eldric said, storming past Lorali and leaving her alone in the doorway with Daeson glowering at her. He stepped forward, but she did not move. Did not back down.

"You were never here," he said, voice deathly calm. "Forget about this place all together."

They stood there, each refusing to break the stare. She heard Eldric shifting, giving a low grunt as he lifted Saraina in his arms and headed back towards them.

"Thank you for saving Saraina," was all Lorali said as she turned on her heel and walked out the open door.

***

Stellian Dumont's house was on the other side of the city, and Lorali didn't think it wise to have Eldric come with her when she escorted the girl home. She watched the too-even rise and fall of Saraina's chest, how her eyes moved beneath shut lids as she tried to get a sense of Lorali's living room.

"Are you going to keep pretending you're asleep and make Eldric carry you home too?" she finally asked between sips of water, brows raised as she looked at the girl expectantly. Saraina's eyes fluttered open with a sheepish grin.

"But he's so dreamy, who wouldn't want to be held in those strong, muscular arms?"

Lorali's vexation must have been evident as she crossed her arm with a stare, causing Saraina to wince.

"Don't tell my dad?" she whispered her attempt at a plea.

"You went too far for that. You nearly died, Saraina, what were you thinking?"

The girl propped herself up on her elbows, movements slow as if testing her tired limbs. Her eyes grew sad, but she tried to play it off with a shrug.

"There's this boy, he was supposed to meet me, but he never did. I—I didn't realize how long I had been out there until that guy came along and helped me."

"Never do this again. You want to meet a boy? Don't slip your guard. Or let me know and I'll help you so something like this doesn't happen again." Lorali wanted to shake sense into the girl but didn't. It wouldn't have helped anyways. "You're lucky that they were the ones that found you and not someone else."

"The goddess must be on my side, since my luck has yet to run out." The girl grinned, earning a light swat from her healer.

"How did they know to find you? Did you put, like, a spell or something on me that says 'if lost, get Lorali'?"

Saraina pushed herself all the way to sitting with a groan and Lorali assessed her for the tenth time that day, worried that she might have missed something and not realized it. Truthfully, Saraina's usual level of inflammation was better than ever. Lorali presumed that's what happened when you had the power of three different gods working to save you.

"Coincidence. A damn lucky one. Be sure to thank Ostara tonight. Thank all the gods, actually. Leave good offerings as penance for the trouble you caused."

"But they could have gotten any healer," Saraina continued, not satisfied with the answer. "But they got you. Why?"

Lorali sighed, lifting her right arm covered in swirling ink.

"Did you hear about this?" The girl's eyes lit with understanding.

"So he's—"

"Yeah."

"And he's—"

"Yes, now stop with that look, Saraina. It's only called a marriage, we aren't actually married. He lives with me for now; hopefully spending forced time with me changes him for the better, and when his time is up he'll leave. That's it."

Saraina's eyes sparkled, excitement brimming beneath the surface as she looked between Lorali and the back hall where Eldric washed the day's sweat and grime off him.

"Oh, how romantic! This is just like something out of a novel!" she squealed quietly, suppressing a smile behind her hand.

"No, this is real life and—" Lorali paused, processing what Saraina had just said. "Wait, there are books about this?"

She had been looking everywhere in the Order's library for some kind of text that had a firsthand account of a gallows bond with no luck. Saraina nodded.

"Mhmm, lots of 'em. The two bonded characters always realize that they love each other in the end but the journey to getting there? Now that's the good part. You wanna borrow them?" She grinned, ear to ear.

Lorali hesitated, unable to believe what she was about to agree to.

Chapter 12

Eldric

Fireflies danced in the darkness, flitting about in pairs with their green-yellow glow illuminating the open window. The throbbing within his chest was ceaseless, and he wondered how Lorali would find her way home—if their separation affected her just as much as it did him. Would she walk with those self-assured steps, her creased brow the only sign of anything wrong? Or would she stumble across the cobbled stone until it turned to a trodden dirt path, finally leading her to him? He'd pushed at first when she wouldn't let him go with her to take Saraina home, but then he agreed that it was best for him to not show up at a council member's house after nightfall with his daughter in tow. His footfalls were the only sound that filled the empty house for hours as he waited for her return.

Left with nothing but his thoughts, Daeson's words from earlier were still echoing against the walls of his mind.

You don't find it strange?

No, he had answered. He knew how involved Lorali was within the Order, spending more time at the temple than at home. They were lucky today was her off day, that her home wasn't on the other side of the city. That she knew exactly who they asked her to save and had the power to do something about it. The guts to take that step against the Order and channel power from deities other than Ostara. It was something he could tell bothered her, a step he didn't know if she'd recover from.

Some would say that the gods had been on their side today, but Eldric knew better. It was Lorali—her competence saved the girl, not any god or goddess. They were useless without her as their conduit, her quick thinking, her capability earned through years of dedication and study.

I trust her.

More than me? Daeson had asked, the years binding them together laid bare in the simple question. Reaching forward, he'd covered Daeson's hand beneath his own.

Never more than you, Daeson, but I do trust her. This was a coincidence—a pure, damn lucky coincidence.

I don't care, I don't trust her! Daeson's whispering grew louder, and Eldric had to squeeze his hand to remind him to be quiet. Lorali was still there, in the room next door, as they continued to argue.

Are you really going to jeopardize everything by trying to keep her here against her will? he asked, knowing Daeson's fear was driving him. Eldric didn't blame him—couldn't blame him. After all that he had been through, suspicion in heavy doses was unavoidable. *That's a good way to get every guardsman in the fucking city looking where they shouldn't be. Guarantees they'll find this house and everyone in it. You can't get rid of her without killing me too. Even if you did, that still has every guardsman out looking for the next archcleric. Do you want to risk that? Or trust that I know what I'm doing?*

And then she'd appeared, as if their voices had summoned her. So innocent, it clawed at his chest to think that Daeson would harm her. Fear did that to people, made them irrational. Dangerous.

His mind spiraled, picking apart everything said between them over and over and over. He went to the garden, pulling vegetables from the soil and freeing them from their stems to add to dinner. He knew the ravenous appetite she had when coming home from a grueling day at the temple and he'd bet his few meager coppers that she had eaten nothing since breakfast.

Strange, he thought, how short and how long three months could be. Long enough to know how she often forgot lunch when out in the garden, lost in the warm loam between her fingers. Short enough that they still kept each other at arm's length. That divide between cleric and convict they maintained with their secrets. She was there, close enough to touch—to feel beneath his palm and know. But he had never tried, never reached out to bridge the gap between them. He hadn't thought he wanted to, until now.

He wanted to know her, he realized. Know her soul, what made her heart beat hummingbird fast within its ribbed cage, the places she hid within herself that no one would find without guidance. He wanted to unravel her and entangle himself in the existence that was Lorali Wynmar.

When the sound of feet against packed dirt mingled with his own pacing steps, Eldric had the front door open in an instant, breathless as he took her in. Marigolds swayed in the night breeze, lining her path with their sweet scent that hung thick on the humid air.

"Thought I was going to have to come find you." He tried to keep his voice light, to hide the way the knot in his throat dipped as he watched the moonlight dance in her hair.

"I told you not to wait," she said, everything about her screaming exhaustion. As she brushed past him, the brief touch of their arms eased his aching head in an instant, a sigh passing his lips.

"I would wait lifetimes for you, Lorali," he said with a lazy smile, following her in. "Plus, it's a little difficult when a magical tattoo makes it painfully obvious when you're not around."

Kicking her boots off at the door and setting down a stack of books, Lorali slumped into the chair, strands of hair slipping through her fingers as she cradled her head with a groan. Shutting the door behind her, Eldric slid the bolt home.

"Stellian was furious—he had the guard searching for Saraina all day. I couldn't leave her there until he calmed down. I knew I'd be late, but I didn't think it'd be this bad." Unshed tears lined her eyes, from exhaustion or pain, he didn't know. As she pinched the bridge of her nose, he decided it was likely both and offered his hand. She shook her head, leaning away from him. As if leaning on him would make her break.

"Lorali, let me help," he whispered, kneeling beside her with an upturned palm still outstretched. It didn't matter to him that their bond was gnawing at his bones, rattling his head, and demanding her touch. If he was in pain, she must be in agony after everything she'd done today.

He didn't like the thought of her hurting when there was something he could do to help.

She glanced at it, hesitant. Almost weary.

"I don't need your help," she whispered.

"I know." And he sat there, waiting for her to take his hand. To trust him enough to let her guard down with him. The moment she placed her hand in his, she gave a sigh of relief, slumping forward and pressing her forehead into his shoulder.

"I'm sorry if I've been hurting you today," she whispered, voice hoarse. "I feel like I'm always the one who pushes the bond to its limits. I'm bad at this whole 'wife' thing, aren't I?"

"Nonsense," he shushed her, running his hand over her braided hair. "You're the best wife I've ever had," he teased.

"Only wife you've ever had, I think. By that logic, I am also the worst wife you've ever had."

He leaned her back with a devilish smirk and quirked brow, a hand on each arm. "Oh Lorali, don't you know you're the only one for me?"

When she looked away with rose-flooded cheeks, it only made his smirk grow wider.

"I think you mean the only one willing to put up with you. Stop saying things you don't mean. It's embarrassing." She pouted, as if she were truly disappointed at the thought.

"What if I do mean it?" he asked, gently guiding her chin so she would look at him. "I've grown quite fond of you."

He saw her swallow, eyes wide as she looked at him. His heart raced as he glanced down at her lips, leaning in. She didn't move to meet him, but didn't move away either as he cupped her face with a smile.

"And I'm beginning to think that, maybe, you've grown rather fond of me, too, Lorali Wynmar. And, as your doting husband, I think it's only natural." He could feel her breath on his skin as he waited for permission, for her eyes to flutter shut, a subtle nod, a tilt of her head. Anything that showed she wanted this too.

She pushed at his chest, whispering his name. He looked up through lowered lashes to find pure panic in her eyes as she said it again, with more force. Demanding his attention. "Eldric."

He sprung back, cursing that he may have severely misjudged their situation, and hurt that the thought of kissing him would put such a look on her face.

Then he smelled it, as she pointed, shoving his shoulder so he turned to see the light grey billow of smoke coming from their oven.

"Eldric! The food—it's burning!"

***

Despite their flatbread laden with cheese and garden vegetables being thoroughly singed at the edges, they devoured it at record speed sitting across from each other on the couch, legs tangled together.

"What do we actually know about the bond?" he asked, reaching over to swap their empty plates for the cups of tea waiting on the side table.

"Surprisingly little," she said, raising the offered glass of sweetened chamomile to her lips, savoring the cool and floral taste. "We know that it is an ancient ritual recognized by the city and, within the faith, clerics are allowed to invoke. We know that it binds the lives of two people together in all ways, intrinsically linking them until the set time is up. We know that the farther apart we are, the more painful it becomes and the only way to get relief is—"

"Cuddle time?" he teased, knowing how it annoyed her when he referred to it as such.

"Physical contact. We don't cuddle," she deadpanned, just as he expected, causing him to chuckle.

"But how does it work? Does it siphon off our innate magic? What if one person didn't have any magic? What then?"

Lorali paused, a flash of uncertainty crossing her face as she watched the remnants of melting ice swirl in her tea, and thought for a moment.

"It was theorized by the Vikal that every person has some level of magic in them. How practical it was to use was a different matter," she mused, a smile crossing her face as she continued. "They were the ones who originally developed lucernas, you know. Supposedly to test a child's magical capability when they came of age. So, if we want to believe that, then the bond would work between anyone—even people with no practical magical capabilities. But I don't know if they're the most trustworthy source—they believed in dragons, and perpetuated the belief that they were the only people who could tame them. Kind of hard to tame a mythical creature, though." She chuckled to herself as if she had told the funniest joke.

"You know the strangest facts," Eldric murmured with a quirked brow, quietly sipping his own drink and listening to the cadence of her voice.

"When you've done as much research as I have, you learn a few things. Even so, I still haven't found any written record or firsthand account that could tell us other important information we may not have discovered yet." She frowned, eyes flickering over to the small stack of clothbound books she brought back with her.

"More research?" he asked, inclining his head. She nodded, her lips pressed tightly together.

"I'm hoping to find some information, or at least ideas, to answer our questions. What's the farthest distance the bond can be pushed? Is there anything that resolves the pain quicker? Are you able to tap into your bonded's magic? There's just so much we don't know."

Eldric sipped his tea, hushed and thinking as he absently brushed slow lines across Lorali's calf with his foot. He could tell she was still exhausted, still in pain. He felt it too, her end of the bond a tired and taught rope that could snap if pulled too hard. He worried that, if they weren't careful, they could cause permanent damage that this slight contact of their skin wouldn't be able to relieve. A simple bandage on a bleeding wound that required pressure. His brows furrowed and his finger tapped a silent rhythm against his cup, mind whirling. Reaching for something he had said months ago, at the beginning of it all.

"Must be why it's called a gallows marriage," he whispered, eyes flashing to her.

"What?"

"Remember when we first found out that this," he placed a hand on her calf, "helped? That we were going to look like an old couple to anyone else. If we don't know the rules, we should work on figuring them out. What if married couple behavior is what makes things better, if we can speed up the process by—"

"We are *not* doing that," she said with such force, it surprised him.

"First, *ouch*. Second, wasn't suggesting *that*. Third—" he paused, words caught in his throat. "I'm sorry about earlier. I shouldn't have done that."

"What are you suggesting then?" Her brow arched skeptically, looking between where their legs touched and him, ignoring his apology. As if she didn't want to talk about it. It was his mistake; he could do that for her.

"What if we can speed up the process with more contact?" he said, shifting his legs just enough that they broke contact and the pain came roaring back to life. "A finger doesn't give as much relief as a hand," he said, a small wave of relief coming from the first touch and intensifying with the second.

"So what if..." He stretched out his hand toward her, motioning for her to come closer. She stared at him, mouth slightly open as if he had asked her to marry him for real. "Oh, don't give me that look, it's possible and you know it. We try this, and if it doesn't work, then we know."

"And if it does?" She winced at the loss of contact as she spoke, the pain springing back to life within his chest.

"If you keep staying late, I really will end up getting cuddle time." He smirked playfully.

Lorali pursed her lips and he could see her mind at work, every emotion playing across her unguarded face. He loved that he was the only one who got to see it. The hesitation between staying put and coming to his side, the moment when desire for comfort won, and the trust she placed in him as she moved across the couch into his awaiting embrace. Eldric pulled her closer, scooping her into his lap so that she could rest her head upon his chest. In an instant, the roaring pain quieted into something sweeter, something domestic. It felt like home—as if they were two parts of a whole, finally put back together. Perhaps they were. Maybe they were now bound, forever intertwined with the other with no hope of ever separating, even once their bargain was done. He could tell she felt it too, her limbs lax against him as every bit of tension melted away.

"Don't try anything weird again. I'm fine with making us both suffer," she cautioned, not bothering to open her eyes. He couldn't help but smile down at her as he brushed a stray piece of hair behind her ear.

"I'd never dream of it."

Chapter 13

Lorali

Sunlight dripped into the living room, filtering through the gauzy curtains and bathing everything in its soft glow. Lorali almost never had the chance to enjoy those peaceful hours when the birds sang their song high in the trees. The sound of her footsteps on the familiar path from home to the Order shushed them as she passed. She'd never realized that a glint of sunlight shone through her window, reflecting off the hanging copper pans in the kitchen across her face, warming her skin and painting the back of her eyelids a warm orange at this angle.

Something stirred within her, a small flame kindled with comfort. With the sound of a heartbeat beneath her ear and the rise and fall of a chest. The weight of a warm hand along her back tracing the grooves of her spine as if it were scripture that must be dedicated to memory. In her sleep-addled haze, she was content to stay in that comforting embrace. She couldn't remember the last time she had fallen asleep in someone's arms. It had been a lifetime ago, and it hurt to feel just how hazy the memory of her mother's touch had become, the sound of soft hummed lullabies beneath the stars. Her heart wanted nothing more than to savor the scent of soil and pine beneath her.

But that was just a memory, a dream of a time long lost to another's greed, and reality crashed around her in an instant. Heart racing, she pushed herself up, trying to make sense of who it was that held her, that touched her with such familiarity. He blinked up at her, surprise lining his clover green eyes. Eldric.

The night before rushed back to her—their bond pulling them together, easing the ache in their bones from a day of magic and distance. She looked down at his sleep-mussed hair, and half-open eyes. Gods, she had fallen asleep on top of him.

"You snore," he said flatly, hand resting upon her back still. She quickly moved, scrambling off the couch, looking at him and the small drool stain on his shirt from how soundly she had been sleeping. Her face burned bright as she looked away, stepping towards the window and seeing the sun rising ever higher within the sky. A stone dropped within her stomach as the temple's bell began to chime from downtown. She counted the tolls, praying that each one that passed would be the last. On the ninth ring, every-thing went quiet.

"Gods above and below," she breathed, running through the house, throwing herself into her bedroom, and slamming the door behind her.

"Lorali?" Eldric called. Concern laced his voice when he only heard curses in response as she stubbed her toe on the bed. "Lorali, what's wrong? Are you okay?"

Quick steps rushed across the hardwood, following her path to the back of the house. Her uniform was dirty and rumpled on the floor since she hadn't had the chance to do the laundry like she planned. She tore every piece of clothing out of her closet, searching for a clean under tunic.

"I'm fine—I'm just—*I'm late!*" she shouted, loud enough to carry through the oak door. She could've cried when she found one, pulling the fabric over her head. Late wasn't a word used to describe Lorali Wynmar, Cleric of Ostara. She had never been late a day in her life. Never missed her duties in sixteen years. For years she had worked hard to uplift her standing within the Order, to show others that despite her young age, she could still excel. It felt as if to be late now would be to throw it all away.

"You need to rest," Eldric called through the door. She could see him in her mind's eye leaning against its frame as he waited for permission to enter or for her to come out—whichever came first. "You were so exhausted yesterday you fell asleep in an instant. Tell them you're sick."

"I said I'm fine."

"Lorali—"

"I get one day off, El, *I'm fine*—"

"Stop saying that!" His voice was sharp, cleaving through her panic in an instant. "Your day off was anything but restful, Lorali. You are not fine. Look at yourself, and tell me otherwise."

When she looked at the mirror, the mirror stared back. Reflecting the disaster that was the room she tore apart trying to find anything to wear. Her breath heaving in her chest as she wrung a gilded over-dress between her hands. Her eyes were almost hollow, dark circles beneath them. She touched her face gingerly, unsure when they got there.

Stopped with nothing else to distract her, she could feel it. The ache deep in her bones, the trembling in her gut that left her fatigued, her throat tight. How tired she was. Lorali could hear his palm rest on old brass, the metal knob twisting slightly beneath his hand as he fidgeted with it. Like he always did when he was waiting for her blessing to enter.

"Can I come in?" It was soft when he asked, hesitant and waiting.

"It's a mess in here," she whispered, feeling the flight that had overtaken her the instant she woke up leave just as quickly. She sank to her knees amidst the chaos, exhaustion running so deep she didn't know if it'd ever leave.

"I didn't ask if it was clean," he amended. "Can I come in?"

She nodded, hesitant. After a moment, she realized he couldn't see her from behind the door. She had to tell him. Her mouth opened, voice stuck within her throat as she searched for the strength to let him in.

The floor was scattered with clothes, desk filled with old cups and bowls and plates from midnight snacks needing to be washed. They teetered in a stacked pile next to the framed sketch of her mother and father she'd drawn when she was young enough to remember their faces without the haze of time, well-worn folds still visible despite being pressed between glass. Outside the sunlit window, their garden bloomed beneath fresh morning dew and bright yellow bees bumbled about the flowers and fruits and vegetables. She touched the necklace that always lay at the hollow of her throat, securing her mother and father's wedding bands close to her so that she always carried them with her, and swallowed. Searching for strength.

Her voice cracked when she spoke, but the word came out no matter how pitiful it sounded. *"Yes."*

The door opened slowly as Eldric cleared his throat, staying just outside the door as if he might spook her into running once more.

"You should take some time away from the Order to recover," he said softly, brows creased as he looked at nothing in the room but her. He didn't care about the mess, how things looked or how her shirt was so twisted within her hands, she knew she'd have to iron the wrinkles out.

"I can't." She could feel unbidden tears pricking at the corners of her eyes and she did everything to hold them at bay as her heart trembled inside her chest, skipping beats as it raced faster than she had ever felt before. Her voice quivered. "There's so much to do. They need me."

"You need yourself more right now." He stepped in, and she flinched. He hesitated, but didn't step forward again. "I've seen you work yourself to exhaustion day in and day out; you are at a breaking point. You need to breathe. To be."

He sank to his knees to be with her, waiting. "You performed a miracle yesterday, Lorali. An absolute miracle. Saraina would have died, but you saved her—poured everything you could give into healing her. Your body—your soul—needs to recover from that. If you keep giving parts of yourself to others without taking time to heal, soon there won't be anything left. You'll crumble."

Silent tears spilled over her cheeks, rolled down her neck, pooling along her collarbone as she shook her head. "I don't—I'm fine. I'm fine, I'm fine, *I'm fine*—" She choked back the sob and kept telling herself that until it was true. Because it was. It would be, one day. But her body knew the weight it carried, the pressure she placed upon herself, and the words were not a balm that would melt into her skin to heal her wounds. They burned along her veins, finding every cut and scrape to seep into and make her feel how not fine she really was.

She held the crumpled shirt in her hands, pulling it close to her chest as the first whimper escaped her lips. In an instant, Eldric was there, pulling her into his arms and allowing her to lose herself in the storm that was her grief. Her anguish. But as her lungs expanded with each hitch in her chest, she could not get enough air. She hungered for it in a way she never had before as her world began to crumble around her.

"Lorali," he whispered, his hand resting against her back, feeling the ragged saw of her chest. "Lorali, it's okay. The work will be there when you get back."

She shook her head. "No—it's not. Nothing is okay, no one—"

Realization capsized her heart, pulling it under as she thought of all she had given and never received in return.

Lorali screwed her eyes shut, trying to block out the chill of panic seeping into her very bones. Dragging her under. One thought echoing throughout her very core. For every cup she filled, no one filled hers in return. In all her years, no one had cared enough to do the same. *No one cared—*

"*No one cares.*" The confession came between sharp breaths, her trembling hands clutching the wrinkled shirt like a lifeline. But even she knew it would not keep her from being pulled beneath the current.

"I care," Eldric whispered, gently cupping her cheeks. He raised her face to him, ruddy and tearstained, and looked into her with such tenderness that she wanted to believe. His thumb brushed away the tears before he took her hands and placed them over his own heart. She could feel it, strong and sure, beneath her palm. The steady rise and fall of his chest.

"I'm here. *Breathe,*" he said with a voice so gentle, she couldn't help but mirror as he breathed in deep through his nose, then out through his mouth. In and out, until it began to calm her uneven heart. They sat there, the warm sun streaming in through the windows as it rose higher into the sky. His eyes never left hers, even for a moment.

"With every breath, you are safe," he murmured in reassurance as he took her palms and placed them over her own heart.

"With every heartbeat, you are strong." His hands wandered back to her face, gently brushing away blonde strands that stuck to her skin, wiping away the remnants of tears and pressing a kiss to her forehead.

"With every moment, you are loved." Warmth bloomed within her cold chest, filling her with hope. Here, in the wreck that was her room, he sat. He stayed. He was there. And she wanted it. Wanted to believe him when he said he cared. Wanted to take his strength and let it fill her, as she had done for others. Wanted to be the person that was cared for.

Leaning forward, she pressed her forehead against his chest. Felt the beating rhythm of his heart, wrapped in the scent of pine and soil that had become an unbeknownst comfort to her as the months passed. Despite it all, how strange their relationship was and how little they really knew about each other, he was an anchor for her to return to. One that she had attached herself to, never realizing she was adrift at sea. One that did not ask for anything in return.

When her sobs eased and quiet hiccups took their place, he still held her tight, chin resting atop her unbound hair. Time passed and she said nothing, unsure how she found herself within his embrace again, but this time she did not run. This time, she let herself be.

Eldric was hesitant when he broke the silence. "So you're not going to the temple, I take it?"

She peeked up, looking at the sun continuing its ascent.

"I don't...What do I even say?" Her voice croaked as she blinked, running a hand through her hair and feeling the spiral of worry begin to pull at her, threatening to unravel once more.

"Don't worry about that, just tell me how you need to let them know. I'll take care of it," he said, palm cupping her cheek as his thumb brushed away the lingering tears.

***

Eldric dictated the words for Lorali to transcribe, taking the fear of saying the wrong thing off her shoulders so she would finally send the message along a phoenix-shaped flame to the archcleric's office. Her impatient feet had worn a fresh path into the floor as she waited for the underwhelming response of *'feel better'* written in Sage's familiar scrawl before the parchment turned to ash atop her dining table. Eldric tried to convince her to stay out for the rest of the month, but she'd refused. She said she only needed the day and he threatened to tie her to the chair. The rest of the week had been the only compromise they could agree on. She needed to be back before the summer solstice as part of her duties for planning Veridian.

And she was glad of it.

Guilt gnawed at her bones, souring the honeyed tea in her hands and muddling her mind when she tried to distract herself with the garden. Just today was enough to drive her mad, mind whirling and fighting for every excuse as to why she should be there. How was she supposed to do this for a whole week? But Eldric still didn't let her step foot toward the temple. Did his best to keep her from thinking about it.

"It's like you've never taken a vacation before."

"I haven't," she muttered, glowering down at her half-empty glass.

"Anywhere. You can go anywhere, Lorali! No one is expecting you at the Order for days. You say the word, I'll make it happen. Promise." He leaned forward, elbows on the table and chin resting in his palms, as he waited for her desired destination. By the gleam in his eye, she knew he would rearrange the stars and their paths just to make it happen.

Brows furrowed, she stared at him, willing some inkling of desire into existence. She loved that spark of adventure in his eyes and the thought of dimming it made her chest tighten. Her mind drew nothing—she had nowhere she wanted to go. Everything important in her life was here on her property. A cozy home, a yard covered in wild berries and flowers reaching toward the sky, someone who understood. Why would she want to go anywhere else?

She paused, considering.

"What about the starberry patch?"

Chapter 14

Eldric

Dawn was breaking over the rolling hills as night still clung to the dew-shadowed grass. Eldric and Lorali walked in companionable silence, morning brews in hand as they relished the morning birds' song. The stars twinkled out, the sun's light sending them to bed until the next evening when they could play once more. It was a balance, a peace inherent in nature that was in constant motion while they passed through underfoot.

"How far did you have to go for those starberries?" Lorali asked, eyeing the pack he shouldered, skeptical as the sun rose higher in the sky and the formidable heat returned. Her green cotton skirt swooshed at her calves, the short sleeves of her blouse puffed out from being tucked beneath dark stays. Seeing her away from the house in anything but her robes was a rare sight that Eldric drank in.

"That patch was near the city gate, but this one is my favourite and well worth the trip. I haven't been in years."

"This is more than just a quick, half-day trip, isn't it?" she asked, hesitant.

"Yep."

"What about my plants! Someone has to water them, probably at least twice a day in this heat—"

"Already took care of it, Lor," he assured her.

"You said you haven't been in years. What if there's nothing there now?" Her mind was already at work, always needing a plan. He didn't stop as he looked at her with raised eyebrows and a half smirk.

"Well, that's why they call it an adventure, Lorali. We'll just have to find out."

***

The sound of wooden wheels on gravel crested the hill behind them and they moved to the edge of the trodden path, giving a halfhearted wave as the merchant cart pulled by a lone mule took the road. Its owner nodded his acknowledgement as he moved past. Eldric watched as the older man turned around to look at them and he couldn't help but keep his hand on his sword's pommel as it slowed in speed and they began to catch up to it.

"Headed toward Juelton?" shouted the cart driver, the brim of his straw hat casting stark shadows against his bearded face when he turned around.

"Yes, are you?" Eldric questioned, shielding his eyes from the sun as they slowed their approach. The man seemed harmless, but then again, most people did.

"Yes sir, sure am. I'd be more than willing to let you ride on the back for a copper. I'm sure your lady there ain't happy about walking all the way there." The man's sun-leathered face was wrinkled with fine lines, long grey beard blowing in the soft hillside breeze.

He met Lorali's smokey eyes with a raised brow. Her freckles stood dark against her pinked cheeks and a thin sheen of sweat had already formed across her brow. While the scenery was breathtaking on foot, the thought of her overworking herself going along with his half-baked schemes made him reconsider. Taking a coin from his pouch in offering, he handed it to the man before guiding Lorali to the back of the uncovered cart.

"You want to trust a random man on the road?" Lorali whispered, looking between him and the cart driver as he came around the back. "What if he tries to attack us?"

"You married a random man at the foot of the gallows, Lorali, I don't think you have much room to talk," he whispered back with a smirk.

She opened her mouth to retort, but must have thought better of it. Lips pressing together, she said nothing. His hands went to her waist on instinct and lifted her into the cart, her stubborn protests mingling with the sound of his laughter.

***

Within an hour they were deeper into the foothills of the mountain range, exploring the packed dirt street lined by the same buildings owned by the same families they had been for the last fifty years, the once vibrant painted exteriors now washed out by years in the sun. While he had grown in his thirty-two years, Juelton still had the same unchanging charm as when he was a boy. A town, frozen in time. It made coming back easy, his favourite haunts as a child the same as ever. Meandering through the heart of Juelton, he took her hand so they wouldn't be separated in the summertime tourist crowd bustling about. Eldric and Lorali looked through the open windows of stores as they passed by, slipping in and out of their doors as they perused. When the smell of warm sourdough wafted through the air making his mouth water, Eldric tugged Lorali to the counter of his favourite cafe in the hillside town.

"Why, Eddie Lorecaster, is that you?" a woman's voice crooned, looking up with a wide smile as the front door chimed. "I'd recognize those clover eyes anywhere. Where've you been, hun?" Her words were slanted, the edges rounded with a mountain accent he had lost to time. He couldn't help but smile at the tall woman who stood behind the counter, her light brown skin tanned from the summer sun and new silver strands woven into her familiar, dark braids. She was older than he remembered, but that kindness crinkling the corners of her eyes was timeless.

"Hi, Miss Marta. It's been a while." He smiled as she reached over the counter and scooped him into a hug, pressing a kiss to each cheek. He couldn't help but laugh at her unchanging personality. Always big, always loud, always warm.

"Well I'll be, Eddie, it's been years since you've been home! I thought you'd gone and died on me. Don't you know how the post works—?" Her questioning came to a halt as she realized he was not alone. Her eyes dipped to their hands, noting the same swirling tattoos that ended in a band around their third finger. "Ah, who do we have here! Did you run off and get married without me and Lou knowing? She'll be mad as a hornet when she finds out!"

"This is Lorali," Eldric laughed, dodging her questions with practiced ease. "We're going to the starberry patch down by the jewel, I figured you and Lou might like some fresh berries in exchange for a bite of lunch?"

"Now Eldric, if your mama heard you trying to bargain with me for food, she'd have my head. What'll you be having?"

"I'll—" he started before Marta promptly cut him off with a raised hand.

"Not you, I know what you're getting. Your friend here, Miss Lorali, was it? What can I get for ya?"

Lorali blinked, looking between the two who only stared at her, waiting.

"Uhh—whatever he's having will be fine. I'll pay for our food—" Her voice was quiet, her hands already moving toward her coin pouch.

"Nonsense, any friend of Eldric's eats here free. It's the least you deserve for putting up with this troublemaker." Marta grinned before waving them to a table and turning to make their food. The cafe was slow in the late morning, those searching for breakfast already gone and those searching for lunch yet to arrive. The perfect time.

"So, you're from here?" Lorali asked as they took the corner table surrounded by windows. Her gaze was pulled to the outside, watching people and carts pass. Though she didn't look directly at him, he knew she was still listening.

"We moved to Athera when I was ten; people in Juelton didn't pay enough for my mother to raise a boy who outgrew his shoes every season and ate his weight in food," he said with a shrug, leaning back to watch the sun gild her pale hair. Her brows scrunched together as she studied him, the slightest hint of a frown playing at the corner of her lips.

"What's with the scowl, Lor?"

"I'm just wondering how much there is to you I've yet to learn."

"Quite a bit, but for you, I'm an open book."

"Really?" she snorted, elbows on the table with raised brows.

"I think we're close enough for that, don't you?" he replied with a soft smile.

He meant it—if she asked, he'd tell her. Despite the fear that she could see him for how little he was worth and flee, he was still willing to take the chance. He would bare his soul to her, and pray that she would keep him at her side when their time was up. He realized these last few days that, already, he didn't know how he would live in a world without her constant warmth he'd grown accustomed to, that glow of goodness that made him feel like he may be worth redeeming, if he could just make her smile. That he had been worth saving at all.

"Then I have to know, *Eddie*," her expression turned mischievous at the use of his old nickname. "What are we having for lunch?"

***

Sunlight glinted off the small lake's surface behind them, a jewel nestled at the foothills of the mountain towering overhead. Though the basket was heavy in Eldric's arms, the thought of meats, cheese, and marinated vegetables between a fresh sourdough loaf was enough of a reward for his efforts. Marta had never made a sandwich he hadn't devoured, and he knew this would be no different. *Fit for a picnic,* she said, passing the basket and giving his hand a reassuring squeeze. With a soft, knowing smile, she sent them off with an offer for dinner on their return and a place to sleep. A grin spread across his face when he peeked into the basket and saw a bottle of cider for them both and small jars filled with enough oils, vinegar, and spreads to dress their sandwiches however they pleased.

They were almost there. South of the jewel hid an untamed patch of starberry brambles that crept through the forest clearings, feeding both wildlife and adventurous children alike for years. He could still remember the sweet taste of fresh-picked starberries on his fingers beneath the summer sun, the feel of his sweaty hair curling in the humid summer heat, and the sound of his mother's laughter as she watched over him, waiting for his energy to run dry. It never did. Only after her passing did he realize how much he would yearn for those days, when the promise of returning together was no longer there.

"There they are!" Lorali exclaimed, spotting the clearing filled with bright yellow berries nestled within green leaves, warm beneath the sun. Gathering her emerald skirt, she sprinted ahead with an astonished laugh. "I don't think I've ever seen this many in one place!"

"Athera's a bit too warm for them to grow well, but closer to the mountains they're like weeds. Delicious, savory little weeds." He chuckled, settling into the grass beside a stacked stone pile at the edge of the clearing, just within the shade's reach. Watching Lorali kneel in the grass, using the fabric of her skirt as a basket to collect starberries for their feast, it was hard to reconcile the sight of her unseeing eyes as she channeled the gods. Something so divine, he feared he might ruin it. But here, in the trees and the wild with the scent of rosemary soap on her skin, she was merely a woman. Something he was beginning to think she never had the chance to be before.

Unpacking their basket, Eldric glanced at the stones beside him, and his throat tightened. Twelve years. He couldn't believe it had been that long since he was last here. There had been so many things to do, a life to live, that he just...hadn't been back. Sometimes it felt like his life here, in Juelton, was nothing but a dream—or that his life in Athera was a nightmare. He wasn't sure which. He had never stopped long enough to figure it out. To merge those parts of himself, the then and the now. Because perhaps, if he didn't, being here wouldn't hurt as much. With a shaky hand, he took a small rock from his pocket, placing it atop a stack that had grown in his absence.

"Hey, mom," he whispered. Eldric rested his chin on his knees, eyes tracing the dark veins within the thick granite stone at the stack's base that marked where she rested.

"I'm sorry I haven't visited." He swallowed, blinking up at the bright sky and willing the sun to dry his tears before they fell. "It's hurt too much until now. To think about you. To be happy. I was so tangled up in my hurt and pain, I couldn't bear the thought. But that's changing. It's a little late, but I think I found someone. I wish you could have met her, mom. You'd have loved her. She reminds me it's okay to keep living. She makes me want to."

His breath shuddered through him and he tucked his head into his crossed arms, focusing on keeping an even in and out as the soft sound of Lorali's shoes neared, stopping in front of him.

"El?" Her name for him was full of worry, the fabric of her dress holding a bountiful harvest of berries for them to share. "Everything okay?"

He nodded, wiping his hands across the grass. She sat down and scooped handfuls of starberries into the now empty basket, studying him as if he were someone worthy of concern. As if she could see every part of him, and still wished to be at his side.

"Being sentimental," he said with a sad smile, divvying up their food. He could see the war play across her face, deciding if she should reach out. To touch. He would not keep it from her; he'd expose his grief to her healing hands if she'd allow it. And she did.

He told her of his mother's death, how at fourteen he had used the last of their money to bring her to Juelton and mourned her as she'd have wanted. Set upon a pyre on the jewel at dusk, he'd watched her ashes scatter to the wind and those that didn't, he collected and brought to the starberry patch started by her grandmother and buried beneath the soil. Honoring all six of the gods in that ancient way of giving oneself to their care for eternity. He gave her final rite himself, bumbling through the prayers she had taught him as a small child and hoping they were heard. She wouldn't have wanted it any other way.

"May I?" Lorali asked after a few long, quiet moments with a gesture to the stones. Her voice was soft, an offering not as a high cleric, but as a friend.

With his nod, she took the dagger sheathed at her side and carved into the soil six interconnected rings enclosed within a double circle. The sigil of the divine in its simplest form, inscribed within the loam. A symbol of nature and balance; of where all things came from and returned to. Ancient as the foothill towns and mountain range villages that connected the continent, where they still worshiped all gods as equals rather than placing one above all others. The wild lands the Order had left untouched.

Her palms touched the dirt as prayer dripped from her lips, soft yet filled with power. He had never listened to the words of the mourner's prayer before, had never heard them as clearly as he did now. They were not words meant for the dead, he realized, but for the living. A prayer of blessing, of peace. The promise for reunion and healing. Not a prayer for his mother, but a prayer for him. To feel his anguish and let it pass.

Silent tears spilled down the planes of his face, that grief raw and untouched after all this time. Pushed down by anger and rage, by an infinite number of distractions to keep the pain away. But with her words, he felt he might begin to heal.

And as Lorali's prayer ended, she looked to him with caring eyes full of hope, arms outstretched in the sticky summer heat of the starberry patch. An offering for touch not needed for their bond. Comfort and connection that Eldric embraced as he began to weep.

CHAPTER 15

LORALI

NIGHT HAD FALLEN OVERHEAD as they finally returned from the starberry patch with a basket full of berries and hearts full of hope. In the unlit town of Juelton, within the rolling foothills of the Euphedian mountain range, Lorali could truly see just how vibrant the stars could be.

Marta and her wife, Louanna, had insisted they stay overnight. It'd be safer to find a cart on its way to the city in the morning and hitch a ride than to make the two-hour walk back to Athera. It seemed Eldric had planned for this when he packed a bag with overnight clothes for them both. Lorali hadn't objected, seeing the softness in their eyes when they looked at Eldric. Although he had been loved by his mother, it seemed like there were two more people who would always see him as his younger self, despite his age. How fortunate to be loved by those outside one's blood. To be known and cared for, for no reason other than existing. A burning weight sat in her chest, a dim ache for something she had once before and still longed for.

Do they know that you…? The question trailed off as they lay down in the soft grass of the clearing as his tears finally dried. Fingers tangled within her own as they bathed in the sun. A touch for comfort, to remind him he was not alone in this world. That she was there.

No, he'd said. *I don't think I could bear it if they did.*

How do you want to explain this, then? Lorali held up their joined hands, inked in their matching bond. He'd avoided the question earlier, but she doubted he would a second time if what he told her of Louanna was even half true. He laughed.

I'm honestly not sure. Any thoughts?

Lorali'd hummed and mused for a moment, ideas empty of anything that wasn't the truth. *Why don't you just tell them we're married?*

She glanced over to find his green eyes wide and watching her, lips parted in surprise, the sun's heat driving color into his cheeks.

Are you okay with that?

Lorali shrugged. *In the eyes of the city, we are. At least for nine more months. Just because we don't have a…traditional relationship, that fact doesn't change.*

Marta and Lou responded with cheers and squeals of excitement when Eldric finally answered the question—*Who is Lorali Wynmar?*

My wife, he'd said, rubbing the back of his neck as the couple pulled them both into the biggest, warmest embrace Lorali had ever experienced. She couldn't help but smile and laugh, basking in their kindness. How they opened up to her with ease, as if she had always been there.

You're good for him, y'know, Marta had said, coming to her side as they watched Eldric and Lou squabble over who was to make the side dishes. Eldric swore he had perfected her potato salad recipe and Lou told him it was impossible. When Lorali fidgeted beneath the kind words, Marta continued. *I can tell. You make him happy, and for that I will always be thankful.* She felt a twinge of guilt after that. While they weren't lying, they were actively deceiving them. It made her stomach twist ever so slightly, but she understood why he would want to keep this, here with them, untainted by the troubles of his life back in the city.

With bellies full and hearts warm, Eldric and Lorali shared the single guest bed, the rise and fall of his chest lulling her into a peaceful sleep. She savored his scent of soil and pine, closing her eyes and imagining what things could be like if all of this was real. A life like this, with him. Outside of the Order. Peace. She ignored the thread of guilt that wove itself around her traitorous heart. Just for the moment, just for tonight, she would be selfish. To want more than the life the Order had given her when she had nothing. She would let her heart be greedy and imagine. That it wasn't just their bond pulling them together and twisting the strings of her heart. That if he ever looked into her eyes with nothing but adoration and leaned in again, she would meet his lips without hesitation and know it was real, even if only for that shared breath. And she'd imagine that, perhaps, he might want the same.

***

They stayed in Juelton for two more days filled with lake water, sunshine, and more laughter than she had ever known. Though the trip had been short, Athera seemed changed upon their return—crisper, somehow, like fresh-dried linen on the summer breeze. She was reminded after many years that life existed outside the stone walls of the Order of Ostara.

Spending time in the home of strangers, hearing their stories and laughter, revived long-buried memories of a time before Athera. Of the first city she called home by the sea, with soaring winds and laughing gulls. A port sentried by the crumbling ruins of a colossal god, his statue long tumbled into the sea, leaving nothing but a pair of large stone feet straddling the harbor opening, broken at the shin.

There were bright times scattered amongst the darkness of her life. Her own personal stars that had guided her till now. The world was not bleak; hope flickered and danced amidst the long shadows her past cast across her future, lighting the way. Driving her to step forward into a vibrant tomorrow.

A wall had been dismantled between them, piece by vulnerable piece, since they were last home. There were still dark, tender parts of themselves left untouched, but she knew in her soul that those would come with time. And when they did, she'd be ready. But for now, winding through the city streets with their idle chatter and a borrowed basket half full of starberries? She cradled that light, settling it within her chest, and letting it take root. If she tended it, maybe one day it could blossom into something beautiful.

Cresting the hill, they followed the familiar cobbled stones that turned to dirt at the end of the street. Lorali searched through the keys on her waistbelt, trying to find the right one to unlock the cottage.

"It's about time you showed up," someone said as she rounded the corner onto her meticulously cared for marigold-lined path.

Lorali yelped, nearly jumping out of her skin as her heart raced. She knew that smug voice, belonging to the only person who visited her since she stopped living at the temple years ago.

"Goddess above, Heinrich!" He'd been hidden by the arching ninebark bushes at the garden's entrance, his wide frame dwarfing the small bench he shifted on.

"The one and only," he smirked, eyes traveling between the two with curiosity. "Came by to see how you were feeling, noticed you weren't home, so I waited around."

"We were out," Eldric supplied, his eyes narrowing at the high cleric.

"For three days? No telling what kind of trouble the two of you could have gotten up to." Mischief flashed in Heinrich's eyes. It dissolved into a chuckle in an instant with a wave. He stretched, standing to his full height with a groan. "Don't worry, I'm not here to discover your secrets and report back to Sage. I just came to check on my friend and have a chat."

The bonded pair looked at each other, Eldric's eyes questioning and wary. She took a steadying breath with a tight smile.

"Could you go put those inside? Maybe make some drinks?" she asked, fingers brushing Eldric's forearm as she turned to him. He looked between the two high clerics, wary, but nodded.

"Let me know if you need anything," he muttered low, so that only she could hear, returning that soft touch before he headed in. Lorali watched as he slipped the basket to the crook of his elbow, searching for the right key to unlock the door. She couldn't help the snort that escaped as he opened all the curtains in the house, letting the light in and making sure he could see that she was okay. Heinrich was quiet as he watched the exchange with a raised brow. The way she smiled, the unbidden rose tint that crept into her cheeks.

"Still not acting as a—how did you put it—married pair?" Despite the teasing tone of his question, she could sense its sincerity in his soft voice. Lorali's face burned as she turned back to find his inquisitive gaze on her.

"No, we're—we're just friends, Heinrich." She couldn't help the way she bristled at the question, still unsure herself what their present—or their future—held. "The bond requires us to be close; it's only natural that we've fallen into strange habits."

"It's okay, Lor. Whatever this is," he said with a wave between her and Eldric, "it's good for you. *He's* good for you. Eighteen years and you have never missed a day, never stayed home sick no matter how much you should have. Oh, the look on Sage's face when they received your phoenix mail!" He chuckled, shaking his head. His smile softened, hands reaching out and resting on Lorali's shoulders with a reassuring squeeze. It did little to keep the gnaw of guilt that creeped back in at bay, her throat tight and stomach lighting with nerves once more. He must have sensed it, in that way that only Heinrich ever did, because she was suddenly enveloped within his arms.

"You deserve time off, Lorali. Much more time than you took, but I'm proud of you for just getting out of Athera and spending time somewhere else—I really am. There's a life outside of the Order, and I think you've finally found it."

Her eyes welled with unbidden tears as he put the words out into the world. That feeling from earlier that had settled within her chest, warming. Hope that she would go back to see the starberry patch, Marta and Lou. Desire to swim in the crystal-clear waters of the jewel with Eldric once more, their wet skin drying in the long summer sun, and learn more about his life, become part of it. To stay.

And in all that vision, all that she yearned for, the Order had no part in it. She now had dreams of abandoning her duties as a cleric for another life. A different one where she wasn't only a High Cleric of Ostara that people only spoke to in their most desperate times. That she could be just Lorali, standing beneath the sun, and finding solace in those closest to her. It tore her to pieces.

She sniffled, hands clutching the fabric of her skirts and her voice thick as she tried to find any way to tell him that he was wrong. That Eldric was anything but good for her, he was a distraction that kept her from her duties. Like she should have. But she could never lie to Heinrich, couldn't fool him with her words. Her voice cracked as she whispered her unuttered truth. "I don't know what I'm going to do when this year is over, Hein."

The tears flowed free and silent then, soaking the collar of his robes as Heinrich pulled her close just as he always had. Drying her tears now as he did during those first long nights in the Order when nightmares woke her drenched in sweat. She didn't know what it was like to have a brother, but she imagined it would have been something like this.

"What do you want to do?" he asked, rubbing small circles into her back. She was quiet, thinking about what to say. What she *should* say.

As a high cleric, her life was devoted to Ostara's guiding light alone. Others had no place. Eldric would leave when it was over, a distraction gone and out of her way. To want him, and to want him to stay, was to disavow everything she had known since arriving in Athera. Her words tumbled out, a quiet tangled mess of thoughts she could not unravel.

"I don't know. It's all new and strange and I don't know what I'm doing. Everything's happening so quickly and I keep wondering—are these feelings real? Or is this another part of the bond I don't understand pulling me to do something I normally wouldn't?" Gathered in his warm embrace, Heinrich shushed her, rubbing small circles across her shoulders as she whispered. "When it's no longer required, would he even want me around?"

"I doubt you have to worry about that, Lor," he whispered. "I've seen how he looks at you—like you put the stars into the sky itself. Given the chance, I think he'll prove just how much there is to live for. To love. You have to trust him."

"What we're talking about is heresy, Heinrich. About me leaving the Order, never to return," she whispered, letting him go. Her fingers brushing the dewy tears from her face.

"I know—I'm surprised by how little I care." He shook his head with an incredulous chuckle. "You've smiled more in the last three months than I think I've seen you smile in the last eighteen years. I have never seen you this happy. This vibrant. You're healthy, Lorali, you're *thriving*. I don't want you to let that go and make the same mistakes I did."

Regret was hidden within his eyes, a thing unspoken between them for years. The memory of her mentor, a young man with braided hair and the brightest smile. How Heinrich's own hadn't been the same since he left. Eldric's voice was the only thing that pulled them both from their thoughts.

"Drinks are done and dinner's on the stove, ten minutes 'til it's done," he called, opening the door and sticking his head out quickly before returning to whatever delicious smell wafted toward them.

The clerics chuckled, composing themselves. Tucking their sorrows back into their hearts and readying for delicious food with good company.

"Think about it, Lor. I'll be there for whatever decision you make." Heinrich patted her shoulder once before turning toward the house, already calling to Eldric and asking if he could come for dinner every night if the food tasted half as good as it smelled.

She stood for a moment longer, his words echoing within her.

You have to trust him.

As she stepped forward, back toward the house that was vibrant and truly full of life for the first time, a sinking realization settled deep within her bones. Trust had always been rare earned, but for him? For Eldric? It was a willing tithe, an offering of devotion that she didn't realize she had already made. And the fear of him leaving gripped her tighter and did not let go.

Chapter 16

Eldric

THE SKIES OUTSIDE WERE darkening, heralding a strong summer storm to drench those celebrating the Summer Solstice. A promise that cold weather would arrive early this year and the winter ahead would be long.

"This is the reason your bond with the high cleric is the blessing we have been looking for. Only they can open the vault, and better yet, she has been chosen as the Sun Bearer, so there will be a reason for her to open it. We just have to wait until the time is right. It's as if Sylvene herself is giving us the circlet on a silver platter." Daeson's eyes gleamed as the pieces of his plan fell into place.

"So this convergence—"

"Conveyance," Daeson corrected.

"Right. Conveyance. During that, Lorali—the Sun Bearer as you call it—is supposed to just... give magic to the land? How does that even work?"

"Yes." Daeson nodded, arms crossed as he leaned back. "Whoever offers their power will receive it back tenfold. It is a direct connection to the divine that binds you to the land. I imagine this is why the archcleric is having Lorali be the Sun Bearer and make the offering since they are vying to have her take the mantle next. It is a right reserved for the ruler of the land."

"But you're planning to usurp her position."

"Precisely. After she opens the vault, you'll restrain her while I complete the conveyance instead. By taking back the circlet given to us by the goddess, and imbuing it with my power, it will be the first step in taking back Athera from the clutches of the Order. After that, it's a bit more difficult."

Eldric gave a slow nod, trying to wrap his head around it all. There were secrets of the Order and the land that he didn't know. Like the fact that Lorali was this Sun Bearer, as Daeson called it. He hadn't known, but had never questioned why she was always at the temple or what exactly was driving her to the brink of collapse. He found, though, that he didn't like the thought of her giving her power to anyone or anything. He had seen firsthand how she would give of herself until she had nothing left. Their trip to Juelton and week of forced respite had eased some of the burden, brought color back into her face and that spark he cherished back to her eyes. He dreaded the thought of her returning to the Order that would ask her to give more. In a way, this plan was saving her from herself.

A bright crack of lightning crossed the sky, pulling their attention as they counted the seconds until the loud rumble of thunder rolled in.

"I should go, storm's close," Eldric murmured as he stood from his seat on the back porch and stretched his legs. Gooseflesh lined his arms, each hair standing on edge at nature's power hanging in the air.

Daeson stood with him, resting a hand on his back to guide him inside with a bright smile. "Stay, you shouldn't be out in this weather. We can put aside our planning for now and drink until sunrise. Watch the storm pass in good company."

Eldric shook his head, clapping his friend's shoulder. "Sorry, Daeson, I promised Lorali I'd walk her back from the Summer Solstice celebrations. Maybe next time."

Daeson's grin faltered as Eldric gave him an apologetic smile.

"Something's changed between you two, hasn't it?" his friend whispered.

Heat rushed to Eldric's ears, the night he tried to kiss Lorali flashing through his mind. He gave a slight chuckle, scratching the back of his head. He never could hide anything from Daeson.

"I see her so often, I guess we've become friends. There's nothing more than that. She's different from others we've known within the Order. You'd like her if you gave her a chance."

Daeson nodded absently, worry evident behind his eyes. He squeezed Eldric's shoulder. "Just don't let it get in the way of our mission."

Swallowing thickly, Eldric could only nod in response. "I won't."

***

"I thought we could make it," Eldric groaned, clothes drenched in the warm summer downpour. Rain fell in thick sheets that made the rogue and the high cleric seek shelter beneath an old tree on their journey home.

"It's just water, it'll dry." Lorali shrugged as she pulled the thin, pale fabric from her chest and tried to squeeze the excess water out of it. They were drenched, fat droplets still falling between green leaves to land in her pale hair. "Besides, rain during the summer solstice is good luck."

Eldric's nose scrunched, brow raised as he turned to her.

"What?" he asked with an incredulous laugh. "How is cold weather and a hard winter good luck?"

"What are you talking about? Rain on the summer solstice means there will be favorable winds and good fortune," she countered.

"Maybe wherever you're from, but not in Athera." Eldric chuckled with a shake of his head as he leaned back against the tree's trunk. Lorali blinked.

"Y'know, in all these years, I'd never thought that it might be different."

White fabric clung to her skin, translucent in its rain-drenched state as she sat next to him, her blue overdress blessedly concealing her torso from his wandering eyes. He averted his gaze, banishing thoughts of what her skin might look like beneath. They were just friends—nothing more. That much had been made clear. She hadn't brought up their near kiss since, so he wouldn't either. He'd respect her boundaries and her wishes, no matter how much it pained or tempted him.

"What other things do you think might be different?" he asked, crossing his legs and staring up at the foliage.

She hummed, thinking, and if Lorali noticed his wandering eye, the look of desire he was sure had flashed across his face, she didn't breathe a word.

"I grew up in a port city nestled along a thin strip of land connecting Korinth to Euphedos. There are probably more differences than I'm able to remember." Lorali chuckled.

Eldric glanced her way, watching her from the corner of his eye as she slicked her wet hair back from her face, brushing water droplets from her eyes.

"What was it like growing up there? Any traditions you haven't seen in Athera?" His curiosity was piqued; the last time they had brought up her past she had firmly avoided talking about it, as if it hurt to think about. But now, nestled beneath a tree with a storm that drowned out all other noise, she breathed in before leaning back and looked up towards the leaves with him.

"I had a few close friends when I was little. We were always getting into mischief," she said with a wry smile, her head tilting towards him. "Running across the beach chasing gulls, screaming into the winds at a cliff's edge just because we could. Daring each other to climb an old statue just so we could watch the boats pass by like we were birds ourselves. I got new cuts and scrapes faster than my mother could heal them."

Even with her soft laugh as she shook her head at the memory, he couldn't imagine a young and wild Lorali when he looked at her now. She was the responsible one, the voice of reason. A steady rock that did not waver or give mischief a chance.

"Summer Solstice was always fun. No one remembers when it began, but the tradition was still alive and well when I was last there. People would make bracelets from bits of rope or colorful threads and give them to those they wished to keep in their lives—like family or close friends—or someone they wanted to know better. It's how children learned to tie their first knots before ever stepping foot on the docks, and to have your arms full of bracelets was a sign of how loved you were."

"But when my powers manifested, it—everything changed so fast." Her voice wobbled as she shook her head, smile turning wistful as a hint of sadness filled her eyes. "It's different there. Magic is detested. At first, my parents dismissed the strange gusts of winds with my tantrums as coincidence. Or how the tide seemed to be called to me when we walked the beach together. But by the time I was seven, they couldn't explain to others how my broken arm healed overnight or the street lamps shone brighter when I asked them to. I was a kid; I didn't know better. By the time I understood and tried to conceal my magic, word had spread. My father lost his job at the docks, shopkeepers denied my mother service, my friends, they...they stopped talking to me too."

The sentence ended in a whisper, the wet fabric of her dress twisted between her hands. He watched as her gaze lingered in the distance, as if she were reliving those memories just speaking of them. Eldric's throat ached as he watched her, all thoughts of drenched linens and failed advances disappearing at her vulnerable honesty that made his throat tighten.

He had thought her pride, her stubbornness, had been the reason for hiding the troubles that their bond was causing for her. Never suspected it was to save him from a familiar feeling she'd experienced far too young.

"When a cleric of Ostara offered my family a haven with the Order in Athera, we left. Then they died, and I was alone. Not knowing what else to do, I joined the Order that promised me sanctuary."

A heavy silence hung in the air, filling the space between them. He didn't offer a condolence or apology; despite their short time together, he knew her well enough to know she wouldn't want it. Instead, he reached into his own heart and offered a connection.

"After my mom died," he started, voice catching. His grief over her death renewed, still that raw wound which was finally beginning to properly heal. "I had nowhere else to turn. Everywhere in Juelton reminded me of her and being there hurt too much. So I came back to Athera, and I...took a position as a guardsman."

She turned to him, bewildered.

"You? A guardsman of Athera?"

"More likely than you'd think," he chuckled.

"What happened?" Her genuine curiosity tempted him to open up and pour the truth into her waiting hands. But he hesitated, thinking of all she had just told him. The clear reverence she held for the Order that took her in, and he knew that, while one day he would tell her, now was not the time.

"Twelve years ago, I was ordered to drop an investigation because the people it incriminated were of a higher station. It didn't sit right with me. I swore to protect Athera, but how could I do that if my hands were tied by those who created the laws?"

His tensed fists relaxed beneath her touch as he looked over to meet her understanding gaze. Eldric placed his own hand atop hers and gave it a tight squeeze.

"That's when I met Daeson and joined his cause. Fighting for what's right within the city. Taking food for the hungry or wealth for the sick and poor. It's my way of continuing to serve Athera."

As they sat there beneath the downpour and offered little bits of their hearts to each other, he hoped that even after the rain ceased and the sun shone once more, they both would feel a little less alone.

Chapter 17

Lorali

E VER SINCE THE SUMMER solstice, Lorali would find Eldric waiting patiently outside the temple, summer sunset steeping the city in its warm hues as cicadas droned around the wooded path. Laughter echoed around them with every step at each other's side, as if their bond had been forged over countless lifetimes and not mere months. On days their gallows bond was strained and they both ached, when their hands brushed and they found a glimpse of relief, she would slip her palm into his. Feeling the warmth of him, a quiet understanding that they were intrinsically intertwined, that small touch a balm for the soul.

Perhaps Heinrich had been right; Lorali could think of no other word to describe how she felt now other than *thriving*, the mask of high cleric crumbling in his presence. With him, she was just Lorali. Someone who forgot her mugs in the oddest places, that would become so focused on the task at hand she would struggle to care for herself. An abysmal cook. A gardener. A procrastinator. A friend.

Hope filled her, a weight lifting as she realized he understood her peculiar ways, and helped maintain the small systems that governed her life. That she could just be. And that in their silent moments, with pulses thrumming beneath the other's touch, she found she liked it infinitely better than being alone. She never knew she craved the peace of being truly known and understood by another until now. Her need for acceptance rooted so deeply she had pruned the branches of herself to please others until nothing of the truth remained but what lay hidden beneath the soil. Then he had found the gnarled parts of her, mutilated beyond recognition, and tended them until she found the courage to grow into something new.

"I have a surprise for you." Eldric blurted the sentence as if it were a confession he was compelled to share.

"Is it a surprise if you tell me about it?" Her eyebrow quirked as she chuckled.

"Why not? We can make our own rules," he said with that lazy smile of his, that she couldn't help but return. "I'm just letting you know there's a surprise, not what it is. That's why it's still a surprise."

"If we make our own rules, then couldn't you just tell me what it is now?" Lorali nudged him, teasingly, as her heart warmed. When Eldric was quiet for a beat too long, she looked up to him and found something she had never seen from him before: nervousness.

"I needed to have something to give you for your birth-day."

Lorali stumbled, tripping across a stray root in the road as Eldric's laugh, full and rich, echoed within the forest canopy, scaring several birds.

"How did—" she sputtered; his steady grip was the only thing that kept her from falling flat on her face.

"I did some digging. Birthdays are public record, y'know," he teased.

Her cheeks colored as she looked down, fumbling with her keys as they walked through the flower-lined path. Before she could take the key out, Eldric had already jogged ahead to unlock the door. Her heart fluttered in her chest as she followed him in, finding their small table covered in coils of red and golden-yellow thread. She stopped in her tracks, blinking down at the supplies laid out like an offering.

"It may not be Summer Solstice, but I thought maybe you could teach me how to make one of those bracelets? You were so excited and I thought it might be something you missed doing, so I thought maybe we could do it together." Eldric's smile was hesitant as he turned around, eyes full of hope. When she didn't respond, simply staring at the present before her, his face fell.

"If you want, that is. If not I get it, I also made a cake—"

"You remembered," she whispered, looking from the supplies and back up to him.

"Of course," he said nonchalantly, shrugging his shoulders as if it were no big deal. "Why wouldn't I remember something you told me?"

Lorali closed her eyes as tears lined them, nodding her head with an astonished chuckle. Until that rainy day beneath a solstice sun, she hadn't spoken a word of the city where she grew up. Hadn't dared to look back on childhood memories that were both happy, yet tainted with pain. Wouldn't let herself believe she missed making bracelets with others like when she was a girl. Without a thought, she reached up on the tips of her toes and wrapped her arms around Eldric's shoulders, face buried in his collarbone as he stooped slightly so she could embrace him. It took a few quiet moments and trembling breaths before Lorali could finally whisper a response without her voice cracking. "I would love to show you."

She recognized the threads and scissors from her mending kit, colors she rarely used. It didn't matter—he could have used her favorite materials and she would still reach across the table, pulling lengths of thread and snipping them with scissors. All that mattered was that he remembered. That she was sitting here with Eldric's calloused fingers holding the first knotted loop of thread. She fumbled with the beginning knots; she hadn't practiced in so long, but the memory of the weaving patterns engraved in her very bones came back to her until practice led to perfection.

His voice was soft and distant as he watched her fingers move, their heads bent together as Lorali showed him how to tie the strands, braided together until the interwoven threads became one. They talked about everything and nothing at all. How their days were, when his birthday was, if they should keep feeding the stray cat that had taken up residence in the woods behind the cottage. Lorali hummed in contemplation when he asked what was next for her now that the Summer Solstice was over.

"There's the autumnal equinox, then wynter solstice. Each night until Veridian, I oversee the cleansing rituals that start on the night of the solstice, helping prepare the space for Ostara's return from Athanasios." The god's name fell quiet between them, and they both glanced toward the bottle of honeyed whiskey on the third shelf.

"Each night?" he asked, the knot of his throat bobbing as he swallowed.

"Yes." She smiled softly as she secured the final knot on her bracelet, unable to help the apologetic wince as she continued. "I've been meaning to talk to you about it, actually. After wynter solstice, I may not be around here often since the rituals are rather extensive. I'll probably stay there most nights rather than walk back by myself in the dark and snow."

They worked in silence for a moment, her words hanging heavy on the air between them as Lorali guided Eldric's hands as he carefully trimmed the strands to the perfect length. She then took the loop and held it steady as he concentrated on tying the first knot, his fingers fumbling slightly over the delicate threads. With her instruction, he found the rhythm that came with alternating threads over and under each other.

"I could come get you," he said quietly, not looking up as the words left his lips.

"I couldn't possibly ask you to do that, but I appreciate the thought, Eldric," she said.

"You're not asking me to, I'm offering. Each night I'll walk you home, just like we've been doing. You deserve to sleep in your own bed. To have some place to go when the day is over rather than spending all your time there." His fingers paused as he stared at her in earnest. She couldn't tear her eyes away from his. It felt like there was more, just lying beneath the surface. A truth that they danced around that was inevitably pulling them closer and closer until, one day, they'd collide. The moment felt too real, too close. Something more than just being known by him. As if she were a breath away from reaching into her chest and offering him her still-beating heart, hoping he would keep it.

"This couldn't possibly have anything to do with the fact that you'd miss me, could it?" Words rushed past her lips before she could think, her mind and heart overwhelmed and needing to put a safe distance between them so she could breathe.

His grin turned wry, the corner of his lips quirking as he shook his head with a snort before focusing back on his work. "You know me too well."

CHAPTER 18

ELDRIC

THE BASEMENT CHILL HAD Eldric crossing his arms, thankful for the sweater he wore beneath his cloak; frost was beginning to bite at night and the leaves had already turned to fire on their branches, soon to crumble into brown ash scattered upon the ground. Candles and lamps lit the reinforced clay walls in flickering yellow light, casting shadows that danced over every surface. The ink-black darkness within the Athera's basement at night had always set his hair on edge, but these days it reminded him more of the gallows noose and the scratch of a dark canvas hood. His breath coming in short bursts, the feeling of unseen eyes lingering upon his skin.

He studied the layers of soil along the farthest wall, searching for words scattered throughout the clay and loam if he looked hard enough. Words he had been trying to say to Daeson these last two months, but couldn't. The timing never right and every rehearsed speech echoing only in the cavern of his chest that tremored, threatening to collapse if the pillar of their friendship was removed.

Regret washed over him in waves as he looked down at the plans and strategies he had crafted laid out before him, encrypted to protect them from prying eyes. He had made them, keeping an oath made long ago to Daeson to see the kingdom of Athera restored. A vow to see the Order of Ostara pay for its sins. All of it in direct opposition to what his heart now yearned for. A garden in bloom, a warm fire, a life enjoyed at Lorali's side. Being with her, seeing how she lived with faith and sure steps, made his resolve waver. Guilt ate at him as he saw that every document detailing the Veridian festivities strewn across the table had one haunting signature at the bottom of the page.

"I've looked at this every way I can, Eldric, but we can't do this without you."

"There has to be a way. Please." His throat was tight. He'd beg if he had to. There had to be some way to keep his oath to them both, an angle they hadn't considered.

"There is no other way. We need you there, beneath their noses. You are the key."

The unspoken truth was there, though. ***Lorali*** *is the key.* There was no other way for them to enter the vault without a high cleric and, as the Sun Bearer, she was their best bet.

Eldric shook his head, lips pressed tight as his hands raked through his hair in distress.

"Why are you so caught up on involving not only me, but Lorali in these plans?" His voice rose to meet his thundering heart.

"There's no need to get worked up. We agreed that this was the right path." Daeson's voice had that edge to it, the one that usually would stop him in his tracks, have him check his temper that still threatened to rise above his training. Eldric's teeth grit together, his own words from months ago stinging.

"You are trying to bring an innocent person into this."

"She is with the Order." Daeson's dark eyes narrowed, statuesque as he watched Eldric.

"She has no reason to be involved."

"I won't do it," he whispered. "I want out."

His breaths heaved as the words left, hanging in the air. He expected Daeson's own temper to spike, for them to fight until nothing but shreds remained of their tapestry woven together through the years. But somehow, stewing in the unnatural silence was worse; Daeson's dark gaze pinning him to the spot as his lips pressed into a firm line. His hands against the table curled into fists as he closed his eyes and took measured breaths—in, hold, and out. Silence. Heavy, suffocating silence.

He stood in it, uncomfortable and sticky like it was summer once again. Clothes heavy with the humid air, clinging to his skin. It was done; there was no taking these words back. Daeson's promise from years ago when he had joined the cause and sought to tear the Order down. If Eldric wanted to stop, he could. Daeson would let him go with no questions. While Eldric had made an oath, he was free to break it when he chose. His friend had made sure that any help Eldric gave, he gave freely. That he could step away at any time. But until now, neither of them had anything to live for except their own whims. No one they were beholden to that hadn't believed in their cause.

Daeson finally broke the lengthening silence in a voice that, while whisper soft, was deafening in the quiet stretching between them. "Do you remember the reason you broke your oath to the guard? Why you deserted your post and began fighting at my side? To bring about justice and restore Athera?"

Eldric's jaw worked, tongue pressing to the roof of his mouth as he struggled to maintain composure. He didn't know if he could trust his voice, if he could speak without trembling in anger and rage. At the past that brought him here, at Daeson for implying he'd forgotten.

He would never, *could* never, forget the raging flames that burned unnaturally bright against the rain. The weight of leather armor and the seal of the city emblazoned on his chest. Captain Sorin's sure voice commanding their squadron to look for survivors as the cart before them burned with flames that never spread. A young girl with rain-darkened hair beneath a tree, unscathed and left with nothing but the soot in her lungs. The feeling that something was not right as he brought her to the Order's doorstep, her silver eyes gleaming with tears beneath the awning when she didn't want to leave him. His gut telling him not to let go, but his orders making the choice for him. He would never forget how she stretched up onto the tips of her toes, hugging him goodbye and whispering the words that would change his life forever.

Who did this to you? he had asked before he knocked on the temple door. It didn't sit right with him; everything seemed so unnatural. Too perfect. Planned. She'd been quiet and dazed; he didn't think there'd be an answer. He was only fourteen with an imagination that ran wild, searching for something that wasn't there. But then she stood up on the tips of her toes after the archcleric arrived to collect her, arms wrapping around his neck as she whispered an answer in his ear before she was whisked away and shut behind large double oak doors. The words that would send him down a path he could never come back from.

The man with the star.

"The fires, the illnesses, the accidents. You were right, they were all connected," Daeson continued, rummaging through the drawer beneath the table. "If you leave, you should know everything. I finally found proof—I found *her*."

His breath stilled as Daeson pulled out a large, brown envelope and crossed the room with deliberate steps. The ridges of the wax seal creating the Order's emblem.

"How?" he breathed, eyeing the envelope as if it would bite him. If he took it, if he opened it, would he be able to maintain his resolve in the face of everything he had been fighting for? His heart warred with itself. Logic telling him that if he took this envelope, there would be no turning back. That life he longed for would be even farther out of reach.

But justice had his fingers tearing the seal, the envelope falling to the floor as he pulled out a file inked in that same emblem that had haunted his thoughts for the last eighteen years. Chill settled over him like a blanket as he opened the file. Narrowing the world to nothing but the very first page, a portrait on top of a personnel file.

Silver eyes stared back, framed in dark lashes and surrounded by freckle-smattered skin. But the hair was not the light brown he remembered that had been darkened by rain. The person staring back had fair hair spun of light, braided into a coronet that kept her long waves manageable while she worked. Fringe that brushed just below her dark brows in need of a trim that irritated her to no end. The same locks he had assured her no one but her would notice.

"What kind of sick joke is this?" His voice caught in his throat, thick with confusion.

"Turn to the back. Look at the first portrait. The records of her arrival at the Order." Daeson's voice was soft as he came to his side, a hand resting feather soft on his back.

Years of reports passed as Eldric tore through the pages, watching as she aged in reverse before him with each portrait. Her light hair gradually turned dark, but those silver eyes remained until the girl he'd left on that rainy doorstep stared back at him, a distant memory rendered in brushstrokes.

Lorali Wynmar, age 9.

Guardians: deceased by design.

Magical aptitude: remarkably strong despite her age. A destined cleric.

<u>*Progress Report*</u>

Conscript from Istarr, Korinth. Sent to the Order in Athera for training. Despite the loss of a cleric in the flames during transport, it was a sacrifice made for the Star.

Surrendered by guardsman Eldric Lorecaster as noted in receiving report, see next page for signature.

Conscript's memory altered to protect the sanctity of the Order.

Instruction proceeding as planned with excellent results.

Report compiled by Sage, Archcleric of Ostara.

Eldric's hands shook. His throat tightened. He could not stop reading the words over and over, though he knew they would forever be burned into him.

Deceased by design. Memory altered. See next page for signature.

"Was I right? It's her, isn't it? She looks just as you described her here. Those silver eyes are piercing, even in portraiture." Daeson tapped the worn painting with his finger, sounding distant as Eldric could focus on nothing else but the roaring in his ears. The questions and regrets pounding within him as he gripped the pages tighter.

"How did you get this?" he whispered.

"I had my contact in the Order go through the personnel files. After seeing her, seeing her powers, I knew something was—"

"You investigated my *wife*?"

Eldric struggled to breathe as the words left his lips, the thought striking his core. Exactly when had he begun thinking of her as his? Or was he hers? He was fascinated by her kindness, enraptured by her heart. Longed to be at her side. But he had never thought of them as belonging to one another until now. In an instant, the realization washed over him, and there was no denying its truth. As if that is how it had always been. How could he be anything but Lorali's when he had let her into the depths of his tender heart, allowed her to plant flowers with such vibrant blooms? When she had done the same in return?

"I have to know every aspect." Daeson's voice was sharp, eyes narrowing. "Every loose thread must be accounted for. After I saw her power, I had a feeling. The goddess works in mysterious ways."

But it was no goddess who manipulated the strings of fate bringing them together. Athanasios had heard her plea. Had saved his life. Bonded them beneath his very hand. Did the god know that this would be the tipping point, the thing that sent him onto a path he might not walk back from? That would irrevocably change him? Eldric swore he could hear the god's deep voice in answer: *Yes.*

"One last time, Eldric." Daeson's voice was low, calloused palms cupping his face with a softness that portrayed all the years they had known each other. Moments where it had been only them and their racing hearts. The uncertainty of evading the guard and the thrill of a plan coming to fruition. Grief and anguish shared for the ones they'd lost. The search for justice as they tried their best to fix a broken city beneath a corrupted faith. "For me."

His brown eyes were deep and fathomless, holding in them every hope they had ever worked toward. He would execute this plan with or without him. With him, they stood a chance. They could expose the Order's corruption and start the city anew. Without him, they'd be caught and sent to the gallows. There would be no high cleric to save them. Eldric closed his eyes with a sigh, relaxing into the touch.

"Okay," he whispered as his heart tore itself in two. "One last time. Then this is it, Daeson. I can't do this anymore."

"Then it's over," Daeson agreed, a small smile on his face and a familiar gleam in his eye. "Thank you, Eldric."

"Of course," Eldric smiled back, weary as his hands raised to rest atop Daeson's. "What are friends for?"

***

As he walked the path back to what had become his new home, Eldric's mind was quiet in contemplation. It was her. It had always been her he was running towards, the hand that guided him even on his darkest nights. Everything he had fought for and believed in until now. He knew then what he had known the moment he saw the portrait of her younger self. He would do this, even if it meant it would be his last action under the night sky. Within the grace of her touch.

One last time.

For her.

CHAPTER 19

LORALI

BLANK PAGES SAT BENEATH her quill. She begged for ink to fill them, for her hand to move. To craft the prayers and rites that must be given as Veridian approached. Everything was planned to perfection; all that awaited was this. The devotion. *Her* devotion. Each year was unique in the blessings sought from the goddess, no two the same. Each rite as personal to the liaison as a fingerprint. It was an act of devotion to breathe life into words, birthing them anew. Creation in its purest form to offer the divine.

Lorali pushed back from her desk, quill settled within the inkwell, and rubbed her eyes. Wynter Solstice was fast approaching, with its falling snow marking the start of months filled with purification rituals, cleansings, and candlelit vigils that would guide the goddess through her darkest night until spring dawned upon the earth once more. Something she had dreamed of doing since her arrival at the Order all those years ago.

She remembered her first Wynter vigil, mere months after her arrival. How the candlelight glowed within the temple halls, the radial crown bursting forth like the sun from Sage's pale hair as their fervent prayers for the goddess's safe return echoed throughout the night. Her hollow chest beginning to fill with hope that the darkness within her own life might fade with Ostara's guidance. Perhaps if she, too, devoted herself, she would know peace.

A lump formed in her throat and, within this sunless basement, she wondered if this is what the goddess's journey felt like. Hopeless and grey as the dim glow from the lucernas ensconced upon the wall. Arms folded upon the table, she rested her head. Eyes closed as she tried to sort her mind, clear it of any distractions, and keep the threat of stinging tears at bay. There was work to be done. She pushed her thoughts to the farthest corner of her mind, willing them to pass. If they lingered, she feared she would fall apart.

It might have been moments, it might have been hours, but when the sound of a throat clearing echoed throughout the basement chamber, Lorali shot upwards as if lightning had struck her. She found the familiar, pale gaze of Sage taking in the papers strewn across her oak desk, the cup of day-old tea that left stains on the ceramic coaster they had given to her as a Veridian gift years ago. *To put an end to the plague of tea rings on my documents,* the note had said in Sage's scrawling hand. Her cheeks flushed with embarrassment at the state of things.

"Archcleric Sage—" she scrambled to stand and bow at the same time, her knee knocking the table. She bit back a string of curses that should never be uttered in the archcleric's presence.

"At ease, High Cleric Wynmar," they said with a staying hand, the angles of their face softening with a smile that did not reach their eyes. "I came to see how you were."

"Preparations for Veridian are going well, I am working on the devotion for the Wynter vigil as we speak." She couldn't help her downward glance at the woefully blank paper that stared back.

Sage nodded, but she could see the way their lips pressed together and knew she hadn't said what they wished to hear. "That is good. Though, I asked how you were doing—not about preparations. The autumnal equinox was over a week ago; it has now been seventeen years since your arrival. I understand that this time of year can be...*difficult* for you, but I wished to honor you for another year within Ostara's embrace."

Lorali felt her chest freeze beneath the words, unbidden memories of the biting chill of rain dampening her clothes creeping out of the darkest corners of her mind that she kept them relegated to. Her heart ached, and not due to the pull of that tether within her chest. The High Cleric smiled with a nod. "Thank you, Archcleric Sage."

"Just Sage will do in private, Lorali. We have known each other for a long time. You are one of the brightest stars in all Athera, perhaps even all of Euphedos."

She dared not move as Sage neared. Their fingers brushed against Lorali's pale tresses as they regarded her, the ever-present hint of disappointment peeking through in their soft, murmured words.

"It is rare for one's hair to change as ours has. It signifies power—being chosen by the goddess. You have a gift, Lorali, one I hate to see wasted when you are destined for greatness. How long will you ignore your goddess-divined path?"

She swallowed, pulse quickening. It had been foolish to think that Sage had moved on when she declined their initial offer to begin training as the next archcleric this same day the previous year. Living within the Order for the rest of her days and working within Ostara's light.

"Perhaps—" she swallowed, breathing steadily as she kept her shoulders square. "Perhaps someone else would be better suited for this honor."

Agonizing silence spanned the distance between them. She thought perhaps she hadn't said it. Didn't get the words out, that they were still stuck within her, or she had said them too softly.

"The position of archcleric is one I offer to you and you alone." Their pale eyes, so similar to her own silver, were piercing. Sharp. Impossible to look away from. "No one else within the Order has shown as much promise. It is the reason I have mentored you personally throughout the years."

A frown lined their face, that hidden disappointment becoming even more apparent. "I would not have permitted you to divert your attention from Ostara to dabble with the other godlings if I had known you might one day not return to her light."

"I have not strayed. But I'm not ready—I have so much to learn." Her voice was firm, but a whisper of doubt tangled within her, her resolve faltering.

But hadn't she? Here she was, a high cleric, having thoughts of a life outside the Order. A life with someone, a desire to love. It had her rejecting the highest honor of the Order: to teach a new generation of Ostara's benevolence and warmth. The tide of her emotions rose bitterly at the back of her throat as Sage's lips turned up into a smile.

"So your answer is yes, but not now."

Lorali's word's were stuck within her, unable to disagree.

"I will give you until after Veridian—when your gallows bond with the thief is complete, we will discuss the next steps. That should be plenty of time to feel more... *prepared*."

"Yes, Archcleric Sage," she said with a bow, the words twisting inside her like a knife as she let them decide her fate.

***

The grey of autumn did little to extinguish the fiery leaves that burned the trees, bright as they were every year when the ground was damp and the nights cold—even in the slanting light that faded into dusk and settled into night. Lorali found herself on the upper hill's crest, the city she called home to her back and the northern road beyond that she had last traveled down seventeen years ago. That she had started with her parents and ended alone. Unable to go home, but not wanting to be anywhere else. Would her parents be proud of who she had become? The wind whispered through the leaves without answer.

Seven days past the autumnal equinox. Seventeen years. That was how long it had been since she arrived in the city of Athera. Since she had last seen her parents. Her throat tightened and it wasn't just the stinging wind that brought tears to her eyes. A dam had been broken since her trip to Juelton, her emotions welling to the surface unbidden and unable to be pushed back beneath the dark waves of her thoughts. They floated, buoys on a raging sea that marked the deepest channels carved within her heart. Attached to something within the depths that she could not dare to broach for fear of never returning to the surface.

She did not turn as she heard familiar footsteps crunching purposefully through the fallen leaves to make her aware of his presence.

"I thought I might find you here," Eldric whispered.

She did not move, glancing up at him with his heavy cloak and two mugs that steamed in the chilling night. Her silence was approval, and he sat down. She wordlessly took her green mug from him, trying to let the floral scent clear her mind, to bring about thoughts of brighter days. He fit into her silence, staring out across the northern road of packed down dirt alongside her.

"My parents died today. Right over there, by that tree."

Her throat was charred as she pointed at the old oak that had continued to grow, much larger than it had been on that rainy day.

"I know," came his soft reply.

"Did Heinrich tell you?"

Eldric's voice was hesitant, scratching within his throat.

"If you'd like to be alone…"

The offer was there, unspoken. He would leave her to mourn them in private, quiet and silent as she had for so many years. Wouldn't ask, wouldn't pry. He'd let it be.

"I think I've been alone on this day for long enough," she finally whispered.

"Whatever you need," he promised, opening his cloak with an arm.

It was an offering she was too weak to resist. Just for now, she would be someone without promises to the Order. She'd pretend that he cared and that she was allowed to care in return. That she could share her burden and that his arm over her shoulder wasn't a temporary thing, but forever.

"We were moving to Athera," she started, giving a whispered prayer of thanks when she didn't feel his gaze.

"I remember the stars were out. They were so bright when we left Korinth, my mother would point out the constellations and tell me their stories from the back of our wagon while my father drove. I loved sleeping beneath the stars, the feel of my bare feet in the grass any time we stopped. There was a new life ahead I couldn't wait to explore. As we neared the northern gate, we stopped to offer someone a ride into the city, to help them get out of the rain. Then he attacked my father and—" Lorali closed her eyes, glad that this part of her memory was fuzzy. She did not know if she could live if she remembered it all.

"There were flames. My mother told me to run to that tree, to hide and not come out until someone found me. So, I did. I sat. I waited. I cried. Quiet, so no one would hear. Then the screams and shouts turned silent. And I keep wondering, if I had just helped, if I hadn't hid, would they still be alive?" She gave a dry laugh, sniffling into the chilled air. "I know it's stupid—I was nine, what else could I have done?"

The stars were hidden by overcast skies and only the final sliver of moonlight illuminated them. He rubbed her arm, soothing her wound that had never closed right, the stitches never fully healing before it was ripped open once more.

"And that's how you ended up with the Order." It wasn't a question. Eldric's lips pressed together into a thin line as she nodded in answer.

"A guardsman took me."

Glimmers of golden magic dance at the edges of her mind, the outline of a young guardsman, gangly with teenage years, pressing her parents' wedding bands into her palm.

One day, you will want these, he'd promised. Silence was all he received in return before they sent her into Athera.

She could only remember the sway of a horse beneath her. The scent of petrichor surrounding them. The solid warmth of a body and the back of the guardsman's cloak draped over her in an attempt to stave off the cold rain, despite her being drenched to the bone. She had pressed her face into his shirt and cried, pretending it was the rain seeping in as she clutched the metal bands tight within her palms. He had let her.

"I'm sorry," Eldric said, his voice creaking. As if her pain was his own.

"It's history," she said, her eyes adjusting to the fallen darkness. "Sad, yes, but history nonetheless. I would not be who I am without it. I certainly wouldn't have met you."

Lorali made to move, the vulnerability of the moment gnawing at her core, demanding she move on. Not linger. If she did, she might not get back up. But Eldric took her hand, holding her there, his eyes meeting hers.

"Don't do that. You don't need to pretend your pain is not there for me. I will be here for you. I will sit with you in this darkness until our tea runs cold and the wind rattles our bones. However long you need, I am here."

Her hands flexed around the embossed mug. Those familiar grooves and ridges she had traced many times before and would trace many times more. And she sat. Leaning back into his embrace, draped in his cloak as she had been another's on this same day so many years ago.

This time she did not hide her tears, pretending they weren't there.

This time, she let them fall.

CHAPTER 20

ELDRIC

ALL ELDRIC WANTED TO do was vomit. Everything he ingested tasted sour and everything he drank settled wrong. It hadn't hit yet. Not until he saw her sitting upon the northern hill of Athera, looking out upon the road. He knew exactly what she was looking at. Exactly what day it was.

It was her. It was Lorali. The setting of the sun over the western crest marked the anniversary of her parents' death. When he had taken her to the church and let her go. Failing her in what felt like the most unforgivable way.

The beginning of the end of his temporary time as a guardsman of Athera. As he hit roadblock after roadblock in his investigation, a girl's voice still ringing in his ears.

The man with the star.

It could have been anyone, it could have been no one. But the glimmer of a truth he now knew reverberated through his bones as those oak doors slammed. He had delivered that girl into the hands of those who'd orchestrated it all. He hadn't thought it strange, at first, how there was a high cleric practically waiting at the door, the papers ready for him to sign. He had never taken anyone to the Order before. Perhaps that was the way it was done. He didn't know any better until years later when he took another young child to the Order's doorstep and the process took longer than he'd expected. When he asked Captain Sorin, he said that Eldric had just been fortunate that someone was awake at that hour the first time.

Only then did he think to investigate further. Uncovering fires that didn't make sense, illnesses overtaking healthy individuals, accidents claiming the lives of guardians. All the children from these incidents were taken to the Order. A feeling within his very soul knew that they were connected, but there was no proof. No clear connection between them except what happened to the children.

It's the law that young children are to be taken in by the Order, Eldric. There is no grand conspiracy, their commander had told him when he continued to bring case after unsolved case to his desk. *Let it die.*

And though Captain Sorin also found it strange, he hadn't fought the order. As he watched one of the most honorable men in the guard fall in line, the realization dawned on him that true change within Athera would not come from the guard. It was then that he and Daeson found each other, the two of them teaming up in hopes of igniting change. A new cause to fight for with a central burning flame.

The memories had Eldric tossing and turning in bed, unable to get comfortable. The truth of what he had done gnawed at his soul as he berated himself.

Why hadn't he told her the truth—that he was there, that he had failed her?

He knew the answer, deep down. And it made him sick. He didn't want her to stop looking at him with that tender gaze that made him feel whole. She would associate *Eldric Lorecaster* with the night everything went wrong.

So, he'd hidden. Like a coward, he hid the truth from her, knowing not only who he was in the puzzle that was her life, but knowing her personnel file sat hidden beneath his mattress and curiosity burned within him to read the rest.

Right alongside their plans for Veridian. When it finally happened and she discovered everything, she would want nothing to do with him. Rightfully so. He was planning to use her to overthrow the Order and claim it was for her sake. To give her a better life than she would ever live within the Order. Undermining her and any semblance of a relationship they may have built, or could ever have. Betraying her trust. She would never forgive him.

He gritted his teeth and smashed his face into the pillow, a scream burning in his throat. Wanting to let out all the rage and anger and fear for what was to come. He cursed the gods who put him here. Athanasios especially, for he must have known it all when he pulled their strings together. It was a cruel fate he had orchestrated. Giving Eldric the best thing in his life, knowing it would be lost when he finally set things right.

So, he did what he shouldn't have. What he knew in his heart was wrong as he lit the candle at his bedside, pulled the brown envelope with the Order's broken seal from beneath his mattress, and began to read.

Chapter 21

Lorali

Lorali ate her lunch in the temple's atrium, enjoying the last shreds of warmth the sun offered. Colder weather had seeped into the daylight hours and before long, she knew that even beneath the midday sun she would see her breath puff into smoke before her. While the sun warmed her body, a creamy soup of potatoes and leeks warmed her soul, fresh baked rosemary bread making for the perfect spoon.

"You have got to get me one of those," Heinrich said as he sat down with his own lunch.

"The soup?"

"No, the husband. Everything he cooks you always looks and smells so—" he gestured into the air, as if that would explain the concept he was trying to get across. Somehow, it kind of did. "—y'know? Meanwhile, I'm stuck with a grain salad."

Lorali chuckled as he stabbed his fork into a piece of squash with a scowl.

"The lunches here aren't so bad. I ate them most of my life and turned out fine."

"Yes, but I have a more *delicate* palate than you. A taste for the finer things in life. Like that soup." He raised his brow with a smirk, the unasked question hanging in the air. Lorali sighed and pushed the bowl over so he could get a taste.

"Tell Eldric next time you see him to make extras and I'll bring them to you," she said with a roll of her eyes.

"When would I get the chance to see him? You'd see him before me." Heinrich dipped a spoon into the soup, scooping it into his mouth with a sound of delight.

"You told him about my parents so I figured the two of you were on speaking terms now—it's okay, Hein." She laughed, rolling her eyes when he froze like a deer who'd been caught. "I'm not mad. He was actually really sweet. It was...nice to have someone with me that day."

Heinrich didn't speak, watching her with careful eyes before he shook his head with knitted brows. "Lorali, I haven't seen him since the day I stopped by your house."

She felt a pit in her stomach and an unnatural chill spread throughout her. Dread filled her as she shook her head with an awkward, unconvincing laugh. "I must be misremembering, then. Forget I said anything"

But as Heinrich leaned forward on his elbows, pinning her with his intense stare, she knew what he said was true. "You're the last person to misremember something. Tell me exactly what was said."

So, she did. She told him—about that day a month ago when Eldric had found her on the northern hill. Letting Lorali believe that her closest and longest friend was the explanation for why he knew the day of her parents' death. It sounded like something Heinrich would do. Even he murmured in agreement.

"But he never confirmed your thoughts?"

"He didn't deny them."

The high clerics sat in silence, Lorali's soup chilled and Heinrich's own meal looking rather pitiful as cold wind cut them to the bone.

"I don't think it's as bad as it sounds," Heinrich offered after the silence had gone on for much too long. Long enough for Lorali's mind to spiral through every scenario and reason she could think of.

"He lied to me, Hein." Lorali's hands were clasped tightly in her lap as she worried her lips between her teeth. "What if he's been using me to get information on the Order? It'd explain why he's gone all the time, why our bond is so painful. Like he's going out to—"

Her eyes widened as she shut her mouth, keeping the words in. *Like he's going to see Daeson.* Daeson wasn't just his friend, but his comrade. She knew that from this summer when she went to that house to save Saraina. She had thought, foolishly, that Eldric had kept his oath to her. That he was a man of honor.

Oathbreaker.

The word whispered through her mind, sneered at her all those months ago. His reaction to it was so visceral. As if she were too close to a truth he didn't want her to see. She felt herself pale, the blood leaving her face as her hands tightened into fists.

"You made an assumption," Heinrich's voice cut her off with a pointed look, knowing the disasters her mind was creating. "He let you believe it. Similar, but still different."

"How did he know it was the anniversary of my parents' death, then? How do you explain that?" she whispered, her hair standing on edge—and not from the cold. The walls she had gradually begun to let down were rebuilding themselves at a rapid pace and there was little she could do to stop it. "Something's not right."

"I don't know," he said, hand covering his mouth as he thought. "You have to talk to him, or you trust him."

"I did trust him."

Heinrich leveled his steady stare at her, unwavering. She saw the knot in his throat bob as he shook his head. The way he always did when he was about to say something she didn't want to hear.

"You trusted him when it was easy. Now, you need to trust him when it's hard."

As Lorali stared down at the whorls on the wooden table, her jaw tensing as Heinrich defended her bonded with such fervor. Her trust in Eldric, which she had given so freely, was wavering as fear crept in, undermining her confidence. Doubt filled her mind as she wondered if she had enough courage to seek the truth. To have his honesty, or worse, another lie. At least for now, it was all in her mind. Theoretical. Potential disappointment was better than being disappointed. She felt the claws of fear sinking deeper into her as she realized she couldn't bring herself to ask.

Her throat tightened and she wanted to run, to flee, to go back to a time when it was just them in the starberry patch beside the sparkling waters of the jewel. When anything seemed possible, when she was just beginning to care.

She couldn't ignore him until their year was over... or could she? Her mind raced with the thought. There was only a month left until the Wynter Solstice, and she would only become busier with preparations until her devotions began. He already knew that she would be coming home at the darkest hours and leaving before the sun. She could endure that pain. It would be easier to handle than a broken heart.

"Lorali." Heinrich reached forward and covered her fists with his hands, squeezing them tight to stop their shaking and pull her back from her racing thoughts with his voice of reason. "Just ask. I'm sure there is a logical explanation. The two of you have something special—don't let your fears ruin that."

She swallowed, closing her eyes to his earnest look. His faith that she could face this head on with courage, while knowing in her heart that she was only a coward.

"I'll try," she whispered.

CHAPTER 22

ELDRIC

With Wynter solstice days away, Lorali's presence was rare. She took meals at the temple, worked long hours, and came home just long enough to sleep before doing it all again. Ink stained her hands and stress strained her mind. A small part of him feared she might even begin staying overnight. He didn't want to think about that.

When she was home, he did all that he could—filled her cup with tea flavored by milk and honey, waiting for her arrival each night while it kept warm on the woodfire stove. Small cookies dabbled with even smaller morsels of chocolate had become a staple in the house ever since he made them when the weather turned cold, and she loved them. A small kindness to paint a rare smile across her face.

The ghost of her presence lingered within the house as the riotous blooms of spring and lush leaves of summer faded with autumn's harvest. Their garden, once plentiful, was now slumbering. His days were no longer spent tending to flowers and crops, leaving him with idle time to fill. Instead, his feet ambled down the dirt road following his traitorous heart that was torn as it worked in tandem with Daeson's own.

With a shudder, Eldric covered his unwashed hair and days' old stubble with the hood of his cloak, breath smoking into the grey winter as the first snow fell. It crunched beneath his boots, shattered glass that could never be repaired. Wind tore against his clothes, cold and unforgiving as it pushed him back. He dug his feet in with gritted teeth, ignoring the sinking pull in his chest, and waited for the winds to pass.

Eldric knew he could turn back, walk the path that took him to Lorali's side where they could figure it out. Together. Somewhere happier, a new life that would let him be. But there was a thread that still connected him to his oldest friend, a bond so different from the dark god-given ink. He stared at the house, with its long shadows and dead grass covered in fresh dusted snow.

Every dragging step taken down this path was betrayal, the noose of his own creation tightening around him. Strangling the new life he had built. A death march. Shoulders curled inward and head ducked low, he ignored his roiling stomach as he walked into the Athera's house and slammed the door behind him.

***

"Only three months left until Veridian and still so much left to do," Daeson murmured, looking over diagrams. "At least you'll be with me following her to the vault for the conveyance. One less thing to worry about."

The scene played out between them—the path Daeson would take to the vault and where he would hide within the lofted rafters while Eldric entered in plain sight at Lorali's side. All while the Archcleric kept the masses distracted above ground, entrusting the most sacred of duties to a protégé for the first time. When her hand touched the stone and her magic surged forth, opening the vault, it would be then that Eldric struck, restraining Lorali and allowing Daeson the opportunity to breach the vault and reclaim what was his by birthright.

Eldric's skin prickled with unease. A sinking feeling settled in the pit of his stomach as he imagined the betrayal in her eyes. Guilt pulled the threads between his ribs tight, causing his hands to curl into fists at the thought of Lorali Wynmar despising him for the rest of her life. Talking through the plan and imagining the different scenarios made it real. He could see the stone surrounding him, feel the damp chill clinging to his skin, hear the hurt in her voice when she asked *how could you?*

He thought the feeling would pass as he settled into old rhythms, or that their sparse time together might ease the pain. But it didn't. She was beneath his skin, whispering at the edges of his mind. Every thought he had was painted with her.

"I don't think I can do this," he finally whispered after all the possibilities were laid out. Daeson sighed, as if Eldric were a child in need of reprimand.

"We've already been through this. There is nobody else. You are the only person who can get close enough to her without raising suspicion. We need every second of advantage that you can buy us by being there."

How much more would Daeson ask for, and how much was Eldric willing to give? He shook his head, lips pressed firmly together. "No, I mean it, Daeson. I can't do this. I can't hurt her. You have to find someone else."

"What about how the Order has hurt her? The other dozens of kids left orphaned due to their whims? The city and land that is crumbling beneath its feet?"

Eldric could see it, the picture Daeson painted that would make him bend to his desires as he always did, with stunning clarity. His face burned as feelings he couldn't name sprang forth, the seam of a dam beginning to burst.

"Dammit, *I said no!*" Eldric seethed, slamming his hands against the table as he stood, breaths coming in ragged puffs.

Silence settled within the basement. While he was hot with anger, a coldness seeped into his friend's bones, his muscles freezing, eyes piercing. He scoffed, shaking his head as he pushed the papers to the middle of the table, leaning back into the chair with a look of disbelief.

"You're choosing her—someone you've only known for a moment—over me? Someone who has been by your side for years?"

"Don't do this, Daeson." Eldric ran his hands through his hair, pulling at the roots as he turned his back on his friend. He opened his mouth, then shut it again as he heard the chair scrape against stone and braced himself for yelling, for anger. But the calm was worse. It frosted over his skin, making him freeze as his friend stepped into his line of sight.

"Can you live with yourself if you let this plan fail? If you leave me to the gallows because you were too caught up in some girl you barely know?"

They stood there, eye to eye, breath to breath. His dry throat tightened, his throbbing heartbeat echoing inside his chest so loud he wondered if Daeson could hear it. How it hurt, how it tore at him to stand here and draw this line. Eldric did not look away. Prayed his friend did not cross it.

"Like I said: Find someone else."

***

The swirling snow fell quietly, his tracks leading from where he left his best friend in a basement filled with treason. The only thing he wanted more than to scream into the subdued night was a steaming cup of floral tea with honeyed whiskey in front of a fire, and Lorali's quiet mumblings at his side as she read whatever tome she had her hands on for the evening. He hadn't realized how much solace he found in their routine until it was no longer there. The thought of missing it forever was un-bearable. The cottage windows glowed faintly from the hearth, no other signs of life within as he unlocked the door. Another late night.

He hung his coat on the rack, breathing in the stillness that was their home as his mind reeled from his fight with Daeson. He hadn't known there was a line he would not cross for him, but here they were. It was her. She was who he could not betray. The oath he could never break.

Rubbing his hands across his face, he felt the weight of it in his bones as he walked to his room. His blood ran cold as he opened the door. Fresh folded linens lay on the edge of the bed, stacked like stones at a river's edge. Splayed across the bed were the contents of the personnel file that he had tucked beneath his bed.

He forgot how to breathe, how to think, how to speak. How to do anything except turn and run across the hall with a panicked knock on her door as he called her name, opening it when she didn't answer. Her dresser was open, clothes missing. The portrait of her parents absent from her desk. Bile rose within his throat, heart thundering in panic as he stood there, mind racing, wondering what to do as he noticed the bracelet with frayed threads that they'd exchanged lying in its place.

CHAPTER 23

LORALI

HER FOOTSTEPS ECHOED THROUGHOUT the temple hall, lit by dripping candles and the slanting rise of moonlight. A bright garland of orange citrus and red cranberries dried from the previous year's harvest wove between boughs of pine and fir that surrounded the altar, the stark white of shed antlers decorating either side. Offerings from each season that had passed since Ostara's last descent beneath the earth present to guide her home, to remind her of the joy awaiting her return.

The dark stain of her bond was hidden beneath white wraps spiraling from her palms, creeping up her shoulder like the vines they hid until nothing remained to show the world that Eldric Lorecaster had ever existed within her life except her aching mind and broken heart.

The pain was still fresh from that day she'd seen the broken seal with the Order's emblem, illuminated by the sliver of light from the doorway—just enough to catch her eye. A deathly calm had washed over her as she recognized the seal and opened the file to find her portrait staring back at her. She flipped through past versions of herself, marking the journey from a frightened girl with dirt-colored hair to a high cleric with goddess-lightened tresses. Portraits of her gradual transformation commissioned by Sage to document the journey.

Lorali's eyes blurred with tears, unable to bring herself to read the words, fingers trembling as she held the file that contained everything there was to know about herself. When she arrived at the Order, when her parents died, her trials and triumphs on her journey to being a high cleric, Sage's bid for her to be the next archcleric. It would all be in there. Everything Eldric Lorecaster—a crook, a thief, a conman—would need to know about her. Betrayal poisoned the soil beneath them and she couldn't think of anything else as she tossed the file onto his bed, the contents spilling out like ink as she ran.

Every bit of her mind whispered to report him; if he had her files, what other secrets of the Order did he have access to? But her heart had screamed differently, begging her not to. Held onto hope that there had to be a reason, an explanation that would make it all make sense. But she didn't know. She couldn't think. And with shaking hands, like the coward she was, she packed everything she needed and left her home in the care of a stranger who she had almost given up everything for. She reassured herself that it was a blessing. Ostara shedding one last piece of truth upon her life before disappearing into the dark night. A last reminder that she should not stray from the lighted path.

Lorali threw herself into the days of cleansing rituals before holding vigil for the goddess. Surrounded by hazy smoke and scalding steam and skin scrubbed red with salt, she thought about anything other than him. Refining her devotion as rosemary oil anointed her skin. While it distracted her, it did not dull the constant pull of her chest. The ache in her heart.

In the months since their bond began, this was the first time she was well and truly without him. There had been times they had been apart, but never like this. Her head throbbed, pounding with the beat of her heart. The pain spread across her face, down her neck. The lights within the temple nearly blinding as she kept about her duties, something to focus on besides her racing thoughts that would conquer her if she stopped for even a moment. Before she knew it, the nights grew longer until finally, Wynter Solstice had arrived.

Flowing white robes veiled her form, her naturally waved hair pulled tightly back from her face. With each step she took, her neck ached from the weight of the golden halo that burst forth like the rising sun balanced upon her crown. Soft sounds of golden chains rustled against fabric, mixing with the soft hum of prayer.

She did not feel herself—dreamlike as she glided across the floor in practiced silent steps while members of the Temple of the Star knelt on either side of her, lining the long hall that had been cleared of its pews to make room for all those who came to bear witness. She knelt before the altar blazing with burning logs of thick, aromatic cedar within a brazier. And as she had practiced, Lorali lifted her hands and her voice in fervent prayer that would last until the sun rose once more.

***

The sun had risen long before Lorali returned to her new quarters within the temple. No longer did she have to share a long, crowded hall filled to the brim with clerics and acolytes. Now, her room was private. Sequestered. Alone. She had hoped exhaustion would overtake her. She had no such luck.

Carefully placing the sunburst crown within its case on the desk, she untied her hair, letting it flow in pale rivers down her back. As she stepped out of the ceremonial robes, she purposefully averted her gaze from the mirror, refusing to acknowledge the dark, arching spiral above her heart. The wrap she wore around her left arm couldn't fully conceal it. She couldn't look. Shouldn't look. It was a weakness; a fresh, unhealed wound that both demanded attention and to be left alone. Too tender to be touched. But like any healing wound, it itched. It sent her skin crawling and she couldn't resist, despite knowing better. Tears fell as she unwrapped the cloth, revealing the dark ink that had been inscribed upon her skin. An unspoken promise that had been broken.

She tried to lie to herself, to attribute her watering eyes to the pounding ache behind her eyes. But it was her heart that had her crumpling to the floor before the mirror, looking at the reminder of hope gained and then so quickly lost. Her throat burned from overuse, sobs coming in silent bursts that caught in her chest. Her prayers to the light mother for guidance had gone unanswered, the goddess dormant in the days surrounding the solstice. She wondered if she ever heard the prayers her congregation sent at solstice or if it was all for naught.

She looked to the thin line of a faded pink scar on her palm as the last scrap of cloth pooled beneath her. Perhaps there was another god who would answer, one who had sent her on this path. Her fingers itched for the dagger tucked into the nightstand beside her bed. The last two times she had communed with the dark deity had been on behalf of another. To seek him out herself, to request his aid while he had Ostara within his grasp, was only something a desperate fool would do. A desperate fool she was indeed as she pressed the biting blade into her palm, reopening the scar as she had on the day she and Eldric first met.

She didn't dare utter the summoning words aloud as the blood flowed through the clenched palm she held over her heart, fearful of someone hearing her calling upon the very god they prayed for Ostara's safe return from. As if he had taken her and she had not walked there willingly.

Athanasios.

Her mind whispered into the engulfing darkness. Like he always had, he appeared. Answering her summons even when her chosen goddess did not.

Little star.

He stood before her, those deep swirling shadows now glittering like constellations were trapped within his skin. As if he glowed with Ostara's mere presence. Lorali did not know if the gods felt emotions as mortals did, but if so, she would swear there was something similar to contentment settled within his heart, a lazy smile pulling at lips she had not seen before. *Dropping the formalities, are we?*

Do you care? She surprised herself at the dryness in her voice. The lack of reverence, as if she weren't talking to an ancient deity older than the soil and the bones buried beneath it. He chuckled.

No, I do not. He peered down at her, curiously. He did not sit upon a throne or stay at a distance but instead stood before her, closer than he had ever been. Lorali looked up at him with red-rimmed eyes that burned from salt.

Why? she asked.

Be more specific. The god's voice was even, a brow raised. Her voice was broken, echoing throughout the darkened corners of her mind.

Why did you make me save him?

I did not make you, he said, a slight shrug of his shoulders as he clasped his hands behind his back, weight shifting to one foot; the gesture was so human it made her forget what he was. *You chose to.*

Anger flared within her at his carelessness, his lack of propriety. His lack of responsibility for what he did to her perfect life. *You told me it wasn't his time. That I had to guide him.*

And you chose to do so. He did not flinch in the face of her anger, did not simmer or stir to respond. As if it were a mere ripple in the waves of his darkness and not a tidal wave of emotion engulfing her, drowning her with each breath.

Why would he do this to me? Why would he make me feel this way? Her voice was hushed, her deepest hurt bubbling forth as her chest shuddered. Pressure built behind her eyes. *Why do I have to go through this?*

The god did the one thing she never expected him to. He knelt. Before her in a swirling pool of cosmos and aether, he was on his knees with her as she sat in this grief that would not let go.

To learn. His dark hand reached out and brushed her cheek as a single tear escaped. *Things are not always as they seem, little star. Perhaps you should look closer.*

She felt like a child again, as if within his starry night she could see her father and her mother. As if it were them comforting her, reaching out through him.

I hate feeling this way. I hate how much it hurts, Lorali cried, fingers pressing into the wound of her palm in reflex and drawing a sharp breath.

Pain is the mark of the living, he said, lips pressed together in a sad smile. She could see his eyes, gilded with starlight, as he smoothed her unbound hair from her face. He almost seemed regretful, as if he wished he could bear the anguish for her but couldn't. *It is an honor to carry hurt within one's heart, for it means that you have cared. You have lived and you have loved. There is no greater meaning to life than this.*

He stayed by her side as she turned his words over in her mind with deep breaths to steady herself. The biting pain in her palm resonated with them and with each repetition, the words settled deeper within her, firmly taking root.

Thank you for your guidance.

Ah, there she is. His lips quirked upwards as he squeezed her cheeks beneath his palms once before letting go.

Apologies for lacking respect in your presence. Lorali's cheeks burned with embarrassment, and she made to bow before him. Athanasios caught her shoulder, steadying her with his cool, burning touch.

Though I know it is your inclination, I prefer the lack of formalities between us. Consider it a courtesy I extend to those who help guide my wife home.

The god winked at her before waving his hand once and the darkness began to disappear. *Now go—you have much to ponder, and I have much to catch up on. I look forward to our next meeting, little star.*

ELDRIC

ELDRIC SAT ALONE IN the cottage before the hearth and watched the logs crack beneath the dancing flames. Lost in the mesmerizing swirls of smoke wafting up the chimney. Lost in his thoughts about how the life he'd begun to build was crumbling. Lost without her.

He knew Lorali had been within the temple these past two weeks, had followed the tug of his heart through the dark-kissed city until it brought him to the double oak doors. He did not knock; he had no right to show up and demand to see her.

What good would an explanation or an apology be to make up for the past? He had delivered her to the temple that night without question, without thinking. Hidden the truth once he learned it. Had planned to take advantage of her, believing it to be a sacrifice for the greater good. Violated her trust when she had shown him nothing but kindness. How could he ever make that right?

He blinked his dry eyes, looking down to the palm of his hand with its white scar that was beginning to fade. It ached slightly with the changing weather as winter deepened its claws into the land. But it was nothing compared to what he had been dealing with since she left. The sharp, pulsing pain wrapped around his head, burying itself into the base of his skull. A constant companion in her absence. One he deserved. But she did not.

The thought of her suffering because of his mistakes had him taking a paring knife from the drawer and anointing it in the hearth's flames until it burned hot. He had never been one for prayer, but he uttered the words he had learned as a child. They were not the ancient ones that dripped from Lorali's lips when her magic came alive, but they were what he had, and he hoped that the fact that he was bound by Athanasios' hand would leave some connection that he could follow. Maybe the god would feel pity for the woman who so selflessly bound herself to an oathbreaker and would free her from this misery. Eldric cried out as the still-hot steel of the blade dipped painfully into the flesh of his palm.

He sat in stunned surprise as his vision began to blur and turn dark, as it had when they were bound, pulled into a realm meant for gods. Somewhere other than his physical body. Power surged through him for a moment, as if the connection had snapped into place. He wondered if this is what Lorali felt when she communed with the gods. Eldric's brows scrunched as he tried to focus, to pull his thoughts away from Lorali's warm touch amid the creeping cold of Athanasios' realm. He braced himself, remembering the feeling of frost spider-webbed across his skin and frozen bones, as if he'd been plunged into the depths of the jewel in winter. But it never came.

His brows furrowed. He wasn't sure how all of this worked, but the feeling had been similar to start. But now instead of frozen cold, he felt the warmth of the hearth enveloping him, a sense of safety washing him in its orange-white glow. But his eyes were open, blinking into a clear sky, as if he were in the clouds themselves. That sharp pain fading into nothing as he heard his name whispered on a breeze.

Eldric.

He turned around and found himself facing a tall woman in a flowing white dress. Her skin glowed as if she were made of starlight itself, white hair and eyes so reminiscent of Lorali's that he thought he might be dreaming. She smiled, as if he'd said the thought aloud.

Who are you? he asked, wary. The woman stayed at a distance, a content smile playing across her face. Her hands were folded together across her abdomen, swollen and taut as ripe fruit. The goddess's voice was feather light.

I am Ostara. She gave no epithet, her name carrying all it needed to.

You weren't who I was trying to reach. Eldric's eyes narrowed, hesitant. How had he ended up in the goddess's presence?

No, I am not. But my hands have guided your path since birth, young Lorecaster.

Eldric snorted, then realized that perhaps he shouldn't laugh in the presence of a god. He did not know how to navigate this. He had seen Lorali's interactions with Athanasios, had some sort of bearing. But the goddess? He was at a loss.

You must have me confused with someone else. I am no believer of yours.

She laughed softly, a warm sound like birdsong in the morning. *Your faith does not determine if my hand touches your fate.*

The oathbreaker did not avert his gaze or let the goddess distract him from his mission. *I have business with Athanasios.*

I know. And I know what you seek.

Hope flickered to life within, leaving him breathless. Would she do this, not for him, but for her high cleric?

Someone who had devoted her life to the service of the goddess?

Will you grant it?

The goddess shook her head. *No.*

His jaw tightened, chest constricting. He should have known; it was foolish to expect the gods to care for the lives of mortals. Anger flared, his voice raising as he stepped forward to make his plea.

Lorali is your most devout believer. She creates miracles in your name. Rather than guiding my worthless life, you should have been guiding hers. Or, better yet, you should have been fixing the corruption within the Order so she could have lived a real life.

The goddess was quiet at his rage. As if he were a child throwing a tantrum and she, his patient mother.

Every step has led you here. Where you are meant to be. This is the right path. Do not stray.

The right path means nothing if you walk it alone.

Yes. The goddess smiled, eyes seeming to light with joy. *You have learned that lesson well.*

A white mist began to move in, the vision blurring as her words hung on the air.

Have faith that your guiding light will return to you. Follow her. She is where you are meant to be.

He gasped, throwing out his hand with a shout as if it would stop her. Before he knew it, he was left, breathless, on the floor of Lorali's cottage with a bleeding wound and nothing to show for it. He tried again and again to call upon the gods, any god that would listen, without answer.

CHAPTER 25

LORALI

THE BITING WIND OF the dark morning hours chilled Lorali to her core as she walked down the cobbled stone streets. She hid within the Order, sanctifying its halls by day and replaying Athanasios' words in her mind by night, unable to sleep. Searching for truth in the old god's words she had first heard four weeks ago. A gnawing feeling within her said that she would find it with Eldric.

The moon had waxed and waned since she was last within the ivy-laden walls of her home and now hung full overhead in a clear sky for the first time since the new year had begun. Light reflected off the snow, stars glittering above and creating the brightest night she had ever seen.

Things are not always as they seem, little star.

The god had been tender and caring, providing her comfort when she could not do so for herself. When she had no one to turn to, unable to tell even Heinrich what had driven her back to the Order's doorstep. When her goddess left her countless prayers unanswered.

It had taken all this time for her to find the map to her courage and follow it. Now every step down the dirt-covered road and up the stepping stone path made the throbbing within her quiet.

Nose reddened by the icy wind, Lorali quieted her chattering teeth and stilled the shaking of her hand, resting it on the handle. She stilled as it gave way beneath her palm, lips turning downward as the door opened on well-oiled hinges. He never left the door unlocked, always checking it at least three times at night before he went to sleep. It was strange as she peered into the warm house and saw Eldric's deep grey cloak on the hook and boots by the door, his sleeping form curled beneath blankets next to the warmth of the fire and a pillow held close to his chest.

Careful to avoid the floorboards that would creak beneath her weight, Lorali entered her house like a thief in the night—which she very well could have been since he left the door unlocked. His forgetfulness was her salvation, since she wasn't ready to face him, and the sound of a turning lock would have woken him. She moved toward the couch, the carpet muting each step and watched as his pinched brows relaxed. As if he felt the same rush of relief as she softly brushed hair away from his sleeping face.

The flickering firelight danced across the planes of his face. It looked hollow—as if these past weeks had taken their toll on him. She shook her head with regret, knowing that she didn't look any better.

Lorali steeled herself as she left him there, stepping silently through the house and ducking into Eldric's room with its small bed and wardrobe that did not match the nightstand. The covers were strewn across the bed, as if he had been unable to sleep soundly. Her eyes adjusted to the darkness and she did not dare to light the candle at his bedside, instead relying on the rays of moonlight that filtered through the curtains. Papers were piled on his nightstand, ripe for picking. Lorali rifled through them, breath catching as she recognized the date of the Veridian celebration. She grabbed the papers, tucking them beneath her arm. There wasn't time to look through them; every moment she spent within the home brought her closer to sunrise, the waking hours when she was needed at the Order. Increased the chance of him waking to find her.

She tentatively stepped through the open door, surprised to find her bed made and sheets turned down. Dirty clothes she had left behind were no longer scattered on the floor, but cleaned and tucked into her wardrobe.

Sitting in a stream of pale moonlight that spilled across her desk was the very folder she had come in search of. The bracelet he had given her during the Summer Solstice sitting atop it, mended like an unasked question. As if he had been waiting for her return, knowing that, eventually, she would come back in search of answers. She hurried, stuffing the folder beneath her arm and headed toward the door, but wasn't able to leave yet. The clarity of her mind and the lack of pain so enticing that she wanted to stay. She breathed in deep, inhaling the scent of burning cedar that warmed the house. Her hand on the door, she hesitated. Unable to help the pull to turn around and sit on the single seat next to the couch. Count the sound of Eldric's even breaths. She waited for goddess knew how long, lost in guilty relief and dangerous comfort. Stared at the folder clutched between her motionless hands that she couldn't bring herself to open.

"Lorali?" A sleep-addled voice caught on itself, confusion clear as it tried to discern reality from the realm of dreams.

Her breath caught in her chest, frozen like a fawn at the crack of a branch. He stirred, hand rubbing the sleep from his clover eyes. Blinking into the burning firelight as he came to realize that this was not a dream, that she was here.

Lorali stood too quickly, making for the door before his feet could hit the ground. Hand turning the knob as she made to escape his grief-stricken voice as he cursed, tripping over the covers that tangled his legs.

"Lorali, wait!"

She didn't look back. If she did, she knew she would crumble. That she would take his honeyed words and offer understanding. Forgiveness that he might not deserve. She needed to be alone, to learn what truths lay within these pages and make her own decision. Give herself the privacy to mourn whatever part of herself she was about to lose.

Dawn crested the hill as she ran into the sun-painted snow that crept through the trees, Eldric's shouts for her to stop growing quieter as the distance between them grew; she ran and did not turn back.

CHAPTER 26

ELDRIC

S HE HAD BEEN THERE. Next to him, while he slept. Had entered the door he left unlocked just for her, just in case she would come home to him. He kicked the barren tree at the end of her drive. He had slept through it—a goddess-given opportunity to set things right, and he had missed it.

Curses left his lips as his breath smoked into the air, cold biting at his nose and snow turning his bare feet into frozen blocks. He felt none of it, turning back toward the house and pulling on socks, throwing on his cloak, and stuffing his feet into shoes. He was tired of waiting. He did not expect forgiveness or understanding, but wanted her to know how truly sorry he felt.

He followed her footprints through the snow, back into the heart of Athera. Even as the trail disappeared on the salted streets that were just beginning to be shoveled by merchants in front of their stalls, he knew where she would go. Where she had been this whole time and he was too scared to follow. His fist banged against the large double oak doors at the front of the temple until an acolyte opened them.

"Greetings from the star—"

"I need to speak with High Cleric Wynmar," he interrupted, not having time for pleasantries.

The acolyte's dark brows raised in surprise at his sudden request. Every muscle tensed as he took in the wild look in Eldric's eyes, the way his chest heaved from running there.

"You'll need to return during our public hours."

"I need to speak with her. *Now.*" He felt himself bristle, ready to barge through the doors. To search through every room in this damned hall until he found her. Eldric shouted her name, trying to pass the acolyte who glanced to the side who tried to calm him.

"Sir, *sir*. I apologize but—"

"I'll take care of this," came a familiar voice that made him pause. Heinrich Holst.

The acolyte looked relieved to see him as he gave a bow of reverence. Heinrich stopped, resting a reassuring hand on the other man's shoulder.

"Apologies, High Cleric Holst—"

"Heinrich, where is she?" Eldric cut off the acolyte who was looking increasingly annoyed. He didn't care. The

High Cleric dismissed the acolyte, who left in a small huff of robes, before turning to Eldric with a raised brow.

"You've known where she is for the past month, yet this is the first time you have come for her—and with such a fuss. Why?"

Eldric clenched his jaw, holding back a retort. If anyone would get him to Lorali—or keep him away—it would be Heinrich. He didn't need to anger the one person who could help him. "It's complicated."

"Well, uncomplicate it for me." The high cleric's brow rose as he crowded Eldric's space and forced them to both step outside. He clasped his hands behind his back, the door still open behind him.

Eldric was torn between rushing in, tearing the temple apart to find her, and following Heinrich, who could lead him to her. He knew in his bones that he wouldn't get far with the former. It pained him to turn away from those double oak doors once more, allowing things to be left unsaid between them. But even now, without knowing where she was, he could tell that he was within the grace of her presence. The splitting migraine he'd had for weeks eased from just their brief time together. He did not trust Heinrich, did not know him. But he had watched over Lorali every day until Eldric came into her life, had her best interests at heart. And he believed that was something he could have faith in.

He followed Heinrich's steps to a courtyard outside, protected by hedged bushes and the sound of a flowing fountain to cover their words. Eldric spoke of things he had not mentioned in years with hushed tones. The high cleric's impassive face never faltered as he listened to Eldric's confession, of his secretly linked past to Lorali that he had only recently uncovered. Of how he broke his oath to the guard and that they had uncovered Lorali's file when they investigated further. He tread lightly as he divulged the contents of those papers beneath the first portrait ever drawn of her in the Order's garb, of altered memories and planned deaths, while avoiding mention of Daeson's plans. Eldric told Heinrich that if he wanted to confirm, Lorali now had that same file with her. Had come back to retrieve it after the initial discovery before Wynter Solstice.

Heinrich only listened, taking in the information until the thief had nothing left to say. The only indication of any emotion was the slight downturn of his lips, a tightness in his jaw. Eldric had nothing left to say to fill the silence that followed, nothing else that the high cleric could know. He watched light palms run through coiled black hair, those silver eyes strikingly similar to Lorali's. He had once thought that, perhaps, they were related by blood. Now he knew differently, that it was a sign of power.

Heinrich hadn't immediately called for the guards and had him arrested, which Eldric took as a good sign. Hadn't been phased in the slightest, just lost in a thoughtful pondering that drove him mad.

"She doesn't know," Heinrich finally said to Eldric, who only blinked in confusion. "If she did, she would never have run from you. That you had the file was a breach of trust itself, not its contents. If I had to guess, she's still worried you've been manipulating her. Has been since the anniversary of her parents' death where you used me as a cover. Do you realize how much I had to talk her down?" Heinrich shook his head. "Why didn't you just tell her and save us this misery?"

Eldric stepped in close to the cleric, voice dropping into a low whisper. "How am I supposed to tell the woman I love I delivered her directly to the person who arranged the death of her parents?"

The words were out his mouth before he realized them, stunning them both into silence as he revealed his feelings. Heinrich's lips pressed together smugly, as if he had known all along. "A touch dramatic, aren't we?"

Eldric nearly growled in response before Heinrich held up his hand. "But I assure you that you worry for nothing.

Lorali harbors no ill will toward the person who brought her here. Quite the opposite in fact."

"Her memory has been altered."

"No, that memory would have been left untouched—it's too insignificant." Heinrich's voice was strained as he shook his head, disbelief creeping past that stoic facade. "Memory alteration is delicate magic. The mind is a tangled web, intricately woven together. Pull the wrong thread and a person can cease to exist, their mind unraveling until there's nothing left. She remembers her life before the Order. Her parents. You. The memory of what happened that night has changed, but not the aftermath. Not the feelings. Those feelings are all her own."

Eldric's breath caught in his throat, the cold having little to do with how he was frozen at those words.

"Despite what brought her to us, Lorali has flourished and grown within the temple. It was her home, her comfort."

"Was?"

Heinrich smiled.

"Yes. Was. Now, her home is you."

Eldric's heart nearly stopped, bursting with joy. "So you'll take me to her?"

"I will see if she wishes to see you. If she does, then yes. But I will not take you unless it is what she wants."

He breathed a sigh of relief. "That's all I'd ever want.

***

The courtyard was small and his pacing steps carried him across the narrow expanse in heartbeats. Faith did little to quell his racing heart and the nervous way his hands clasped behind his back, fidgeting with each step. It had been well over an hour since Heinrich left. Half of him thought maybe Lorali didn't want to see him. Or that Heinrich was trying to convince her. If she hadn't read the document before, had she read it now? What were her thoughts? Did she hate him as much as he hated himself?

Shouts and the general drone of the city filling with its daily crowd became a buzz, the sound of birds chirping overhead and the lull of the fountain doing little to settle him. His hand rubbed over his mouth, a long exhale as he tried to calm his frantic heart. Clearing his throat.

When the bells chimed the hour, he would go find him. Or her. Or both. He was tired of waiting. Had done enough of it these last weeks. It had done nothing but test his patience and bring him misery. He had thought Lorali didn't want to see him, but she did. She had stayed beside him for goddess knew how long while he slept. If there was any sign that she did not hate him, it was that.

His mind was made up with a plan, determination coursing through his veins. If Lorali wished to never see him again, he would stay away. Stick to the shadows of her life and never approach her light again. All she had to do was say so. They had been through too much together to part without a final word, without decidedly knowing how their year would end. Resolve washed over him, and just as he took a step out of the courtyard alcove, he saw members of the guard patrolling. Old habits died hard, and he turned around to head the other direction only to see more guards.

Sudden realization hit him. This wasn't a patrol. This was an ambush. He cursed to himself, returning to the little protection the hedge offered. Besides the temple, those were the only ways into the city crowds. Eldric gathered his breath, steeling himself, shifting from toe to toe as he prepared to run out of the courtyard.

"I wouldn't try, Oathbreaker," came a calm, almost whispery voice that had grated on his nerves the very first time he heard it. Flowing robes concealed their form as Sage appeared.

"You took something of mine, and I wish to know how."

His heart was within his throat, eyes frantic and wild, palm twitching as he decided if he should just rush past or if he should accept the confrontation.

But pure horror soured his stomach as Archcleric Sage held up not the folder of Lorali's life, but several papers with underlines and scribbles in the margins, a diagram that he had drawn recreating Daeson's maps. His own plans for Veridian he'd been tinkering with at his desk, trying to find a way to keep Lorali safe. He hadn't encrypted them before he went to sit by the fire and fell asleep next to the warm blaze.

The world turned from beneath him as guardsmen surrounded him in the courtyard. He put his hands up, fingers laced behind his head as he kneeled, waiting for the all too familiar bite of metal against his wrists.

He was shoved downward, a knee pressing into his back as a familiar, sneering voice curled hot into his ears.

"I knew it from the start," said Fulke as he finished handcuffing him, wrenching his head backwards by a handful of hair. Forcing him to look at him. "An oathbreaker like you will never change."

Chapter 27

Eldric

THE CELL HE SAT in was cold and damp.

The shadows were empty.

There was no sunlight.

Lorali did not come to see him.

CHAPTER 28

LORALI

HER TEARS WERE LONG dried, leaving her empty within her chambers with nothing but the file of her life. It was the one thing she managed to hide from Sage before they entered her room unannounced, to find her with Veridian plans annotated in someone else's hand. Everything had moved so fast then; Sage calling Heinrich to alert the guards and place Eldric Lorecaster under arrest.

I'm proud of you, Sage had said, cool hand cupping her cheeks as they placed what should have been a comforting kiss to her brow before sweeping out of the room. *Stay here; I will take care of everything.*

Rather than proud or safe or cared for, Lorali felt hollow as she sat on the floor of her chamber. Staying as she was told. There was nothing she could do; it was out of her hands. Eldric would be arrested and sentenced to the gallows, and she would follow. The cold draft that came from the darkest edges of the room ruffled the papers beneath her bed. Seemed to whisper to her, *look. Not everything is as it seems, little star.*

Before another heartbeat could pass, she was on her knees reaching beneath her bed and pulling out the file. She finally read the words written within, pouring over her triumphs and failings. The first rite she performed for a man destined for the gallows, earning her robes when she achieved her status as a high cleric, the early years of her devotion. Lorali's life passed before her eyes in words. All the way back to that very first day. The last page tucked behind a portrait that she almost didn't recognize as herself. She couldn't remember the last time her hair had been so dark. Before her powers, bursting like starlight, began to slowly drain the color until only her pale strands remained.

The pages stilled in her hands as she read a familiar scrawling script she had learned to decipher years ago. She felt the world turning beneath her, mind swimming as she read those words over and over again until finally she had to set the file on the ground, hands clasping over her mouth. Controlling her breath to keep from retching as those words echoed in her head.

Deceased by design. Deceased by design. Deceased by design.

It overshadowed everything else in the file, weighing on her. Dwarfed the realization of just exactly how Eldric knew the anniversary of her parents' deaths or even that her memories had, in some way, been altered. Her mind raced until it finally went numb, and that numbness crept into her bones.

It was written in such a casual yet bold manner, as if no one else would ever read this report that had been locked away in the archcleric's archives for nearly two decades. Her skin prickled with gooseflesh as she began to make connections. Pulling the threads that tied the fabric of her and Eldric's lives together, crafting a seam of new understanding.

There was an infiltrator deep within the temple—someone high enough to have access to such secure files. Though she couldn't think of who it could be, she did know without a doubt who had orchestrated all of it, and she knew where she must go.

***

Lorali's breath trembled as she made her way through the dark street, feeling the tug within her chest as she left Eldric far, far behind while she navigated the outskirts of the East district. Following the road until she reached a bridge that sent fire through their bond as she pushed at its limits.

Pulling her cloak closer, Lorali came to the house that would have once been quaint, perhaps even nice, but was now surrounded by dead grass and chipping paint on the wood siding. All color and life in the estate from the summer sucked into the greyness of moonlight and snow.

With sure steps, she strode to the doorway and slammed her fist against the wood relentlessly until she heard footsteps across creaking floorboards.

"What the fuck?" came a disgruntled growl behind the door, the sound of the deadbolt twisting before it opened. Daeson's hair was mussed with sleep, a tired look in his eyes that only showed a hint of surprise to see the high cleric staring back at him with fire in her eyes. Tracing down the length of his exposed chest was a deep, white scar mottled at the edges. She blinked, recognizing the telltale signs of a magical injury. And from the way it stretched across his skin, it must have been one he earned long ago. Lorali swallowed, bringing her eyes back to his. A spell like that should have killed him. Being within the Order, she often forgot that not all magic was used for good. A naivety she could no longer afford.

Daeson fumbled for that mask of arrogance he held in place for all the world to see, but he could not hide the dark circles that were etched beneath his eyes. The weight of a leader about to burn out.

"You are the last person I expected to see."

"Eldric has been arrested for treason," was her only response, face carefully blank as she watched him. Rage flared behind his eyes as he weighed his options. Careful. Calculating.

"You wouldn't be here if you were the one that turned him in."

"No, I wouldn't be."

"Have you read your file?" he asked with a tight voice. His hawk-like eyes watched her reaction, the way her muscles stiffened, her bottom eyelid twitching just slightly when she worked her jaw at his tone. From the look on his face, he knew it all. Had likely read every word before he handed the file to Eldric. She felt exposed as she realized that a stranger she couldn't stand knew everything about her.

"Yes."

"And?"

Lorali clenched her fists, fighting the urge to snap at him. They couldn't afford to waste time. Her past wasn't important right now.

"I'm here, aren't I, Prince Daeson Athera?"

Daeson's breath froze, eyes narrowing as they trailed the dark cloak draped over her Order-issued attire, the tight braids pulling her hair back sharply from her face.

"Did Eldric tell you?" There was anger there, his defenses high and ready to strike at a moment's notice, but also sadness.

"No, I'm observant," she said, chin tilted back so she could look up into his dark eyes. To show that her fire matched his own.

Without another word, Daeson turned on his heel and left the door open as he retreated up the stairs with a wave. "Knock your boots. I don't want to clean up puddles in the morning."

Knocking the ice-crusted snow from her boots on the doorstep, Lorali stepped inside and shut the door behind her. A log snapped in the crackling fireplace within the living room, the same one where she had saved Saraina months ago. She rubbed her arms beneath the cloak, keeping her feet on the old blanket laid in front of the door. Moonlight reached across the worn floors, mixing with the flickering firelight and casting everything in pale, moving shadows. It made her skin crawl.

"Too damn cold outside," he grumbled, pulling a sweater over his head as he descended the stairs, heading into the living area without a word to her and stoking the flames with iron tools. Lorali followed but kept her distance with the threadbare couch between them. She didn't know if she should speak first, but the growing silence ate at her. Anticipation clawed at her skin, gnawed at her bones. The waiting made her want nothing more than to be planning. Doing. Saving.

"What happened?" Daeson's shoulders were tight as he stoked the fire. "I would have thought your bond would protect him from such a fate.

"Our bond is not protection. If anything, it makes the line he walks thinner." She frowned, fingers tapping against the couch as she tried to maintain composure. "He is under scrutiny, but even if he wasn't, your plans that he brought into my house were enough to get him sent to the gallows once more."

Lorali's cheeks flushed as she looked toward the window. She felt shame coursing through her for having taken the papers in the first place. If she hadn't, if she had just talked to him, none of this would have happened.

Daeson scoffed, turning to stand to his full height.

"Believe it or not, Eldric had a life before you. He's a grown man who makes his own decisions and plans."

"You put him in danger—"

"And you didn't?" His voice rose over hers before he scoffed, shaking his head and placing the red-hot tools back in their place. "You said it yourself. You made the line he walks thinner, put him under scrutiny. And judging from the guilt written all over your face when I answered the door, there's more to the story. You're probably the reason he was arrested in the first place. Am I wrong?"

She could feel all her worst habits coming to light. Digging her heels in, staying in an argument until she had the last word. Proving she was right. She needed to focus on the problem at hand, not dive into it with Daeson.

"None of this matters. What matters is that you need me, and I need you."

"I do not need you for anything," he snarled. The familiar prickling of magic seeped into the air. As Daeson stalked towards her, the wind outside howled, its response to his flaring power. "You are with the very same people that killed my family and stole everything from me."

"And they killed mine as well!"

Unbidden tears sprung forth at the words, rage and disbelief warring within her heart over the truths she had learned. "The archcleric had my parents killed to get my power. You don't get to lecture me about what lengths the Order will go to—I am now well aware since you decided to drag my past out of the archives."

The two of them breathed heavily in the silence, some understanding snapping into place. She closed her eyes, pressing her lips together as she tried her best to salvage what she had come here for.

"We can either sit here arguing until sunrise or find a way to save Eldric and get the circlet of Sylvene. Your plans are obsolete; the Order will be on high alert. You'll be caught and executed. I can't get Eldric out on my own. To get what we both want, we need each other."

He eyed her, likely weighing the risk of trusting her versus the benefit of having her on his team. Then, Daeson exhaled heavily into the night, lips pressed together as he gave a firm nod and gestured for her to follow him. She fell into step beside him as they descended into the basement.

CHAPTER 29

ELDRIC

HIS WEEKS PASSED IN meager meals at guard change and the occasional escort to an interrogation room. Only kept alive so that Lorali could finish her duties because, once begun, the rituals could not be taken over by another. Or so the archcleric had claimed.

He was escorted beneath the ground through familiar passageways hewn from grey stone, flanked by a guard on either side. Even with time between now and his life as a guardsman of Athera, Eldric knew these halls as if they were his own veins. Had patrolled them, escorted prisoner after prisoner through them. The catacombs were disorienting, a maze of dead ends and looping turns. His younger self would have scoffed at the idea of him being the one escorted down these halls in rattling shackles. How disappointed he would have been to see what he'd become.

Slumped in his seat, Eldric waited for Fulke or one of his ilk to begin another day of questioning that would get them nowhere. Eldric never answered straight—or refused to speak all together—causing Fulke to fumble and lose his composure. His tantrums were childlike, down to the uncoordinated thrashing of fists he called a punch. It was a script they repeated over and over, without fail. One he deserved. Though he couldn't help finding a morbid spark of joy at the thought of being able to drive Fulke's arrogant ass to the edge until his last breath. He would make this as difficult as possible, going out kicking and screaming as the door beneath his noose dropped.

When the door finally opened, Eldric's gaze didn't leave the whirling patterns he traced on the table. It was a new form of entertainment, something other than the mesmerizing flickering of the torchlight on the cracks in his cell wall. Someone cleared their throat as they pulled the chair across from him and sat down. The timbre was too deep and rich to belong to his usual interrogator. They rested their large, gloved hands on the table, the city's crest embossed upon the worn leather protruding into his vision. His tracings paused as he looked up to meet the hard gaze of Commander Sorin Nightingale.

"You've decided to come to interrogate me yourself, then?" Eldric asked, putting on a bravado he didn't feel. He knew he could never goad Sorin the way he could Fulke or the others. The man was as solid and unwavering as his faith in Athera. "Did Fulke give up already?

His former Captain—now Commander—gave a grunt of acknowledgment, always a man of few words. Eldric swallowed softly as they held each other's gazes. He knew that, within his heart, Sorin was a good man. He believed in order and rules and justice to a fault. To the point that he could not ignore those things for the greater good, for the sake of the very people they were charged with protecting. Following the law, even though it was wrong. Protecting those who did harm rather than the ones who needed it most. That was not justice.

He tried to sit in the heavy silence, to match the calm of his former captain. But being in his presence broke something in Eldric's armor. A desire to reach out, to give Sorin the chance to do the right thing and investigate further. While he might die, that didn't have to be the end.

"I found it," Eldric finally said.

When the commander didn't respond, he continued. "The proof. The truth. I told you I would find it, and I have. I—was right." His voice cracked at the end. He was right, he thought again as he shook his head with a halfhearted chuckle.

"But at what cost?" the commander asked. There was a soft sadness in those brown eyes of his. One that made Eldric grit his teeth, the shackles at his wrists jingling as he pushed back in his chair.

"Someone once taught me that the price of justice is never free."

"I think you misconstrued my words," Sorin snorted, recognizing his own words from the lecture he gave every batch of new recruits. The one Eldric had heard when he'd been nothing more than a tangle of gangly limbs and bright dreams. Hope undiluted by pain.

"No, I think I learned just what I needed to." Eldric pressed his lips together, arms crossed as much as the bite of the manacles would allow.

"You're a good man, Eldric. It was tragic when you were caught the first time; I'm heavyhearted to see you here again." He hesitated, shaking his head. "There will be no high cleric to save you this time."

"I know."

Eldric swallowed, chest too tight and tongue pressed against the roof of his mouth to keep from biting back. He tried to ignore the weight of his sins that would pull Lorali down with him. If he thought about that for even a moment, his execution would come early. He would be a body without a soul, spirit broken at last.

"What are you really here for, Commander?" he couldn't help but ask, trying to move on from the thoughts. "You sound almost remorseful to have me, your most wanted, in custody. Surely you didn't come to lament my fate."

"Your high cleric asked me to bring this today." Commander Sorin reached into his pocket, pulling a bracelet woven of red and gold. It was Lorali's tidy work he set in the center of the table, cut from his wrist when he was taken in. It reminded Eldric of warm summer days filled with laughter, exchanging their bracelets beneath an endless sun for her birthday. Now, on his own, she returned that very bracelet to him. It tore something within him as he reached forward, not wanting to let the commander see.

"Is this your angle? Try to be sympathetic and get me to talk?" Eldric bunched the braided threads tight within his fist.

"Why did you break your oath to the guard?" The commander ignored his question, bringing up a past he could never escape. "You have still been devoted to justice since you broke your oath. I have watched you serve this city from the outside. Why leave? Why not stay, become the change you wish to see? It's what I've done. The guard differs from what it once was."

Sorin leaned in, fingers steepled as he continued his inquisition. As if he were a friend, that mentor he had been once all those years ago when Eldric was young.

"Not enough, or I wouldn't be here. Everything can't be changed from within. It doesn't happen by following the rules. Ignoring those who are hurt because you are ordered to."

"This is about the girl, still? After all this time?" he asked, rubbing the thick stubble along his jaw.

"It has always been about her," Eldric said. "She showed me that the guard would break its oath to the people by turning a blind eye when ordered. That is not justice. I may have broken my oath to the guard, but I never broke my oath to the people."

CHAPTER 30

LORALI

VERIDIAN ARRIVED AS IT always did: received in a riot of colors and hope—new lives beginning to blossom. She kissed the forehead of the first daughter of spring, a baby girl brought into the world with the rising sun. A sign of luck and prosperity for her life ahead. The bundle of fabric was quiet and alert, new eyes seeing for the first time. Lorali couldn't help but smile at the parents—a fair woman that had labored within the temple since the previous dawn, accompanied by a tall man with muscles hewn from farm work. Though his hair was dark, she could see a glint of red in the scruff lining his jaw and the same bright blue eyes that matched their daughter with her shock of red hair.

"The audacity of babes to come out looking just like their father when their mother did all the work." The woman chuckled, tired but smiling as she touched her wooden amulet, smoothed with age at the edges. "Ostara has returned to us this day. We know she walks among us with you as her mortal vessel. Blessed Veridian, High Cleric. Thank you.”

Lorali couldn't help but smile, taking the woman's offered hand and leaning down to press a kiss into her cleansed palm in blessing. “May everything you touch be blessed, may starlight guide your steps.”

Her face glowed as she received the blessing meant for new mothers who walked through life with freshly barren wombs and an armful of joy. To protect them in the lifetime to come. The woman and her husband bowed once more before heading off, eyes full of love for each other and their newborn baby girl.

Exhaustion swept over Lorali in waves. She had prayed until the candles burned to nothing but dripping wax and low flames, only to be replaced once more to guide the goddess back from the dark reaches of the night.

But when she had emerged from the depths of the temple, guilt made its home within her when the smiles and fervent requests for prayers and blessings came from the gathering people of the city. Her pale tresses and the sunburst halo crowning from her head invoked the goddess' likeness. She was meant to be an inspiration of hope for the year to come, a reminder that even in the darkest night, there is light. A representation of Ostara among them.

Her throat tightened as she stood freezing in the crisp morning air, trying to savor the fresh scent of spring. She didn't want to set foot outside. Wanted to turn back, run through its winding corridors to find Eldric. To do anything other than present the image of their beloved goddess before betraying the very temple that had anointed her.

Heinrich stepped to her side, hand touching her back lightly as he cleared his throat. Without a word, he gave her the strength she needed to step forward, as he always did. She was duty bound, and every step through the parting crowd and wave to the citizens of the city was hope given to them. She couldn't take that away from them.

She could hear it before anything else—the city was alive, dancing and singing with its celebrations and pennant banners adorning every corner, painted in different hues of blue and intricately decorated with the eight-pointed star of Ostara. Weaving through its people with city guards parting the way, she stepped into the open carriage that waited to parade her about the city. With every turn and twist of the stone streets, she felt that persistent tug in her chest, drawing her back to a cell deep within the catacombs beneath the city. That familiar pain, a strange comfort, reminding her she was not alone.

Waves of nervousness crashed over her like a storm brewing off shore. She glanced down at the gauze concealing the dark marks of her bond that might reveal themselves from beneath her long, flowing sleeves. Hidden like shame. An unspoken promise that she would come for him.

As the sun rose higher and Lorali had a moment to slip away, she pulled parchment and ink from her writing desk. The scent of ink filled the air as she dipped her pen, small and careful script effortlessly flowing across the parchment imbued with magic. She folded it three times before igniting it with a spark of her power. The letter went up in flames, the fire twisting and turning, resembling a fiery phoenix in flight. The words seared through the air as they traveled towards the recipient;

My dearest Saraina...

Chapter 31

Eldric

H E KNEW SOMETHING WAS coming from the shiftiness of the guards and how his cell had been scrubbed to remove the grime. After weeks of brewing in his own filth, he was finally given a rag and bucket of water to clean with. It was no surprise when the Archcleric glided in on soft, floating steps in their usual flowing garb, somehow glowing even within the dim dungeon light.

He didn't say a word. With daggers in his eyes and burning hatred in his heart, he fixated his gaze on the archcleric from the corner. The strings that pulled every mysterious fire and sudden illness he'd investigated tied right back to the person before him.

The archcleric's hands were clasped primly in front of them, looking down their straight nose that matched the angular planes of their face. Pale hair and eyes that he now realized were a sign of the magical power leaching into them, making the person into a conduit. Eldric wondered what parts of themselves they had lost in exchange. If Lorali could ever recover herself.

"Who are your conspirators?" the archcleric finally asked, breaking the silence. It was clear from their icy glare that they were a person who was not used to being ignored.

Eldric chuckled, shaking his head. "Wouldn't you like to know."

The corner of Sage's mouth ticked upwards at his reply. "Yes, that is why I'm asking."

"I'll tell you exactly what I told the guards." He leveled a stare at the cause of so much pain within the city. He leaned in close, placing emphasis on each word. "No one."

"It's a shame that your arrogance will be the downfall of such a bright star when all this could be avoided. As your bonded, High Cleric Wynmar will have to suffer your fate." Sage tsked, shaking their head.

Eldric stiffened at the tone in their voice, the gleam in their eye that made him pay attention.

"To enter a gallows marriage is to entrust your life to the other. A promise before the gods to forfeit your life if you fail to reform your partner. There is no avoiding this; there is no saving her." The words were acid, burning Eldric's throat as he spoke.

"You're right—she is the one who chose to save you, promised to reform and reintegrate you into society. You are her responsibility. A responsibility she failed."

Lorali had done anything but fail him. She was his reason—beginning to end. It had started with her, before they even knew it. And she had saved him, changed him for the better. The thought of him pulling her brightness from the weave of stars in the sky was soul crushing. He couldn't blame her for turning in the incriminating evidence she had found—it was her job to protect the faith. It was her duty to report. He had been careless enough to get caught. Arrogance indeed.

"There is no one else," Eldric repeated, forearms resting upon his knees as he attempted to temper his rage before rising to stride toward the archcleric.

"I have been trying to root out this corruption for years, and I finally found the evidence I needed. Right beneath my nose," he sneered, grabbing the cell bars as he spun the story to pin all of the blame upon himself. "Do you remember me? That night in the rain when a young guardsman brought a little girl to you, having no clue that you were the one who orchestrated everything."

Unfazed, Archcleric Sage continued to wear their maddeningly impassive expression as if nothing had been said at all. "You and High Cleric Wynmar will be hung at the gallows together at nightfall at the end of the Veridian celebrations. A truly fitting end to your shared story, don't you think?"

Eldric knew the archcleric was bluffing. Trying to sink beneath his flesh, a splinter wedged just enough to spur him into talking when there was something he knew that could save her. The archcleric had done too much work, pulling innumerable strings to place Lorali at the precipice of power only to let her fall short. Had to know something he didn't. But a deep, paranoid part of Eldric knew that if he called this wrong, it wasn't just his life at stake—it was hers. Sage knew that Eldric would do anything to avoid her sharing his fate and he hated it. He hated even more that it worked.

"Lorali knew nothing," he rasped. "I used her connection to the Order to further my plans without her knowledge."

"I know." Their expression softened with a mix of sadness and disdain. As if Lorali's pain and betrayal were their own. "I've never seen such despair within her before. It has left her hollow."

Guilt curdled in his gut and Eldric looked away from their scrutinizing gaze.

"What would save her?" Eldric asked. "I know there is something or else you wouldn't be here. I will do anything."

And he would. He meant anything and more. If there was one last thing he could do to save her, he would lay himself upon the sacrificial altar if it meant she could live one day more.

"Severing the bond."

Eldric couldn't help the snort of laughter that escaped him. He didn't know much about the realm of gods and magic, but he knew that it couldn't just be undone. Had learned that himself just a few weeks ago when Ostara herself denied him.

"That can't be done." His brows knit together as he watched the archcleric's expression, surprised when the corner of their mouth ticked upwards into a smirk.

"But can't it?"

Eldric's heart stuttered, nearly stopped. They were serious.

"What do you know?"

"The god that bound you can sever it by claiming your soul. Your soul will be lost within the twilight for eternity, but she, as the petitioner, will be spared."

As if the mere mention of the god was a summons, an icy breeze drafted through the cell, making Eldric clench his teeth as his fingers gripped the metal bars, leaning in.

"Then my soul be damned. It is hers anyways."

Sage raised their brows, but nodded.

"I will begin to make the necessary arrangements."

When Eldric didn't respond, Sage made to leave, but glanced back over their shoulder. Disdain was painted across their features as they looked at the criminal within its cage, an animal awaiting its execution.

"You did not deserve her."

They said nothing else as they walked out of the dungeon. Eldric's words echoed into the empty, dank cell. Unheard, but true.

"Nor did you."

Chapter 32

Lorali

FOOTSTEPS ECHOED OFF THE high chamber walls. Lorali was deep within the winding bowels of the temple, the vault settled deep into the very earth beneath the city. Sage was above giving a sermon to the citizens about the year to come while she was within the vault, completing the conveyance. Or so they thought. She couldn't help looking over her shoulder, afraid someone would follow her, knowing she was about to break every rule she had ever learned. But no one did. With a quickening heartbeat Lorali approached the vault door, sealed shut and attuned to the magical signatures of only the arch and high clerics. To anyone else it would look as if it were another part of the neverending stone walls in the basement. But those who knew where to look knew better.

Placing her hands against the stone, Lorali focused her magic, willing it to merge with the stone and unlock the door. She had only been inside once before, after she was ordained as high cleric, to attune her magic to the vault itself. It had taken days of etching her power into its crevices, convincing the magic to accept her. It still took time now to coax the fickle old thing open. Time she didn't have.

Her eyes were closed as she poured all her focus into the door, trying to open the locked vault with its sharp, needle-like magic. Once Daeson freed Eldric, it wouldn't take long for guards and Sage to figure out what was happening. Her time was limited and the faster she completed this, the more time she and Eldric would have to run and escape Athera.

The wall rumbled beneath her palms, magic finally settling into the stone. Light traced a path, spreading and seeping through the carved grooves and illuminating the dark hall. She stepped back, watching the stone shift and move until a perfect passageway, just big enough for her to enter, opened.

Breathtaking—that was the only word Lorali could use to describe the vault as she stepped inside and the rock shifted closed behind her. Water dripped from stalactites, sounding like rain as it fell into the deep subterranean lake. Iridescent crystals were scattered within the stone, refracting light like glittering stars in the lucerna glow, like the stellanium crystal inlaid within her bracers.

Lorali hurried down the narrow path to the lake's edge, nose wrinkling at the smell of burnt matches and sulfur that only got stronger as she neared the water's edge. Each breath came from her mouth, trying to avoid the off-putting stench as she saw the narrow strip of raised stone she was searching for up ahead. A bridge, high above the lake and supported by only a few thinning limestone pillars, connected the tight spiral staircase before her to a rock formation in the middle of the water. It stood tall against the test of time, the resting place of the Sylvean circlet for all these years since the Order usurped the Atheran government long ago. A shiver ran down her spine at the thought. This place was beyond ancient. It was timeless. A rare beauty, one of the few remaining caves in the world with an abundance of the iridescent stellanium crystals. A place that had been stolen for nothing more than power.

Her footsteps were steady and sure as she ascended, hand running along the stone on one side as she climbed to the top of the spire. Nausea roiled over her as she glanced back toward the ground and out across the thin stone bridge with nothing on either side but a long drop into the deep green water. Her mind raced, imagining what horrors awaited within it if she fell below. Even if there weren't any, one slip and it would just be broken bones and water filling her lungs. Her life ending in failure before it ever really began. Her inner voice tried to calm the fears attempting to take root, to soothe them before they grew.

It's not that bad, her mind whispered to her instincts, trying to shut them down.

But you shouldn't be doing this. This is wrong, they whispered back. A stone dropped into her gut as all the doubts began to flood in at once. Everything she had been pushing past for weeks to get to this moment came crashing down on top of her. The danger, the betrayal, turning against everything she had ever known—

Lorali pressed her hands into her face with a frustrated groan as she shook her head.

"No, no, no, no—*focus,*" she told herself. She tried to fight the thoughts, push them away as she always did. But her heart still raced, her mind still whirled, her breaths came in quick puffs as if she could never get enough air. Panic sank its claws into her mind, searching for purchase and not wanting to let go.

Lorali was rooted to the spot, so terror-filled that she could only fall to her knees. She pressed her fists into her eyes and just struggled to breathe in through her nose, breathe out through her mouth.

In, out. In, out. Breathe, breathe, breathe.

Her heart still raced but her mind cleared enough to think back to the last time she felt like this, with Eldric in their warm summer months. How he had placed her hands upon his chest, over his heart, and breathed with her. The words he had said for her until she was okay once more.

With every breath, you are safe.

Her chest shuddered as she placed her palms over where her own heart lay beneath her robes, voice croaking as she whispered. "With every breath, I am safe."

Her voice felt weak; even she didn't believe what she was saying. But some sparking ember lit within her chest, some remnant of his warm embrace. As if he were with her.

With every heartbeat, you are strong.

Salty tears streamed down the planes of her face. She did not brush them away as she rose on her knees, clutching the fabric as she stood. "With every heartbeat, I am strong."

Looking down the length of the narrow stone, her breathing calmed as she acknowledged that yes, it was dangerous. Terrifying, even. She had every right to be afraid. But she could not let that fear control her. She was strong enough to listen to that fear and channel it into something new.

With every moment, you are loved.

Lorali neared the edge of the landing, to where it connected with the stone bridge. Pebbles crumbled beneath her feet, cascading down from the edge. The cavern was filled with a long silence before the sound of a distant splash broke the stillness.

"With every moment, I am loved."

She took the first step.

She looked down to make sure her feet did not miss their mark and tried to ignore the depths below. Scared and afraid, her mantra became a rhythm.

"With every breath, I am safe." *One more step*—the stone beneath her feet was narrow and slick. Her shoes had little grip and threatened to slide beneath her weight.

"With every heartbeat, I am strong." *One more step*—and with a steady breath, Lorali spread her arms out to keep her balance.

"With every moment, I am loved." *One more step*—as her words echoed off the stone cavern walls.

With one wrong step, she would plummet. But that would not happen. Death was not in her future. No matter what obstacles came her way, she refused to give up.

She would not allow it.

Chapter 33

Eldric

*T*HUD.

The sounds of something large hitting the door to the dungeon and shuffling of feet startled him from his dazed stupor. He would recognize the sounds of a skirmish anywhere. Eldric's heartbeat quickened as he scrambled to his feet, hating that he was trapped within a cage and at the mercy of whoever was trying to break their way in to reach the only prisoner in this section: him.

He had nowhere to run, nowhere to go. Still, he moved to a shadowed corner, pressing his back flat against the stone outcropping. Any advantage was better than none, especially with such underwhelming odds. Here, at least, he was hidden at a glance until the intruder passed him. The reflection from a shining shield mounted on the wall gave him a way to track their movements when they entered.

Muffled shouts turned into soft gasps, then silence. Long, dreadful silence. Until the sound of metal tumblers turning inside the lock clicked into place and the door slowly opened. The figure entered, their tall, distorted reflection dripping in a dark grey cloak with a hood pulled tightly over their head. He caught a flash of rich brown skin peeking through where his gloves and long-sleeved shirt met. Eldric's teeth clenched as they searched up and down the cellblock, unable to see him at first glance. He slowed his breathing until it was so soft, his chest didn't rise or move and not a sound escaped. He watched the intruder inspect each cell, searching for him before cursing in a low rumble.

"Eldric," the man hissed. He froze at the sound of a familiar voice. "Eldric, you fucker, where are you? There shouldn't be any places to hide in a damn prison."

The prisoner whirled out of the darkness, facing the intruder. Familiar brown eyes, dark brows, and russet skin greeted him from beneath the hood, the rest of his face obscured by black cloth. But Eldric would know those eyes anywhere, would know that voice no matter the time apart.

"Daeson?" he squinted, as if what he was seeing wasn't real. His voice raised to shout but he caught himself and whispered. "What are you doing here?"

"Great to see you too." Daeson rolled his eyes as he flipped through a ring that held so many keys, it jangled as he flipped through them searching for the right one. "I'm breaking your sorry ass out. C'mon. We have a job to do."

Eldric felt the color drain from him as his best friend unlocked the cell door and stepped inside with him. They were quiet while Daeson searched for the keys to the cuffs that suppressed Eldric's magic.

"I'm not doing the job," Eldric murmured under his breath, backing away with a shake of his head.

"Not this again, El. We don't have time—"

"Haven't I done enough?!" he seethed, unable to control the way his voice rose. Daeson's brows pinched as he tried to step toward Eldric, who dodged him.

"She is going to die because of me. I can't do this job and then leave her to suffer the consequences of my actions. Not when I can save her." He shook his head. "I won't do it. Not unless Lorali is safe."

"I know." Daeson's voice was sharp as he lurched forward, grabbing Eldric by the chain connecting his shackles and pulling him close. Daeson's fathomless eyes were searching his own, glistening as he whispered. "That's—that's not your job anymore."

A puzzled look crossed Eldric's face as he tried to make sense of what Daeson meant.

"Who do you think is helping me free you? How do you think I got the keys to this entire building?" Daeson's chuckle was dry as he shook his head. "Did you know that girl she saved, back in the summer, was the daughter of a councilman? And that they are so close that when Lorali says to meet, there are no questions asked, there are no guards? Kaela has the girl right now and in exchange for her safe return, I get these. I free you. And Lorali brings me the Sylvean circlet."

White hot anger blazed through Eldric as Daeson freed the shackles binding him. He reached forward and took the former prince by the collar, pushing him back against the stone wall he had just hidden behind. His fingers singed holes into Daeson's shirt, his magic running wild for the first time in weeks.

"What did you do to force her—"

"I don't force people to work with me," Daeson snapped. "You know that. *She* came to *me* with this plan. Like hell I was going to pass it up."

Eldric's breathing was ragged as he searched Daeson's eyes for any sign of a lie, but all he saw was truth. Eldric released his friend, who smoothed out the wrinkled and singed fabric of his shirt and cloak with a smirk he couldn't see but was evident in his voice.

"She's a clever girl, that one. Now, if you're done, we need to get—"

The dungeon door banged open, and they both jumped, turning to find Fulke stumbling in with a busted lip and bruising eye. He jerked forward, yanking the alarm rope. Alerting every Atheran guard in the city that their prisoner was trying to escape.

Daeson cursed beneath his breath, an unnatural wind stirring the stagnant dungeon air as his magic flared to life. His words came quickly, decision made in an instant as he turned to step past Eldric. "She'll be at the summer house. Find her. I'll meet you there."

"No, I'm not leaving you. We'll get out of here. Together."

Daeson took his shoulders, squeezing them tight as he shook his friend. Sadness tinged his eyes, showing his age for the first time in so long it took Eldric by surprise.

"Yes, you are. You have a job to do: *keep her safe*. She's waiting for you. *Go*."

Without another word, Daeson stepped out of the cell and a burst of wind threw Fulke against the wall. Daeson rushed him without another word to his friend, grabbing the guard's collar.

"I've been waiting for a long time for this," he ground out as his fist connected with the guard's face. The unmistakable crunch of cartilage was the only sound Eldric heard as he rushed out the door to find the woman that saved him.

***

The twists and turns of the sprawling catacombs seemed endless, but his training in the Atheran guard helped him navigate them with ease. He followed the small markings on the lucerna sconces, their faint glow illuminating the path back to the temple, ducking into their flickering shadows when guards streamed past, heading towards the dungeon. His chest ached, but he was not torn between running back to help Daeson and staying on his mission. Eldric knew what he must do.

An invisible string tethered him to her, and even without Daeson's advisement he would find her again. Always. Something stronger than the gallows bond tied them together. They had found each other time and time again against impossible odds. From when they were young and lost in the rain, to the gallows where they reunited. They would always find each other.

Eldric emerged inside a storage room, and listened before he eased the door open and looked down the empty halls. She was still here, inside. She had not made it out yet. Every hair along his neck stood on edge, every sound readying him to fight as he followed the pull toward the heart of the temple, easing open the side door they had once entered together, back when it all began. Sunset filtered through the skylight, making the stained glass glow in brilliant oranges and reds that set the empty pews ablaze. He slipped through, shutting the door behind him with practiced quiet. She was here—in this room. But where?

With quiet steps, Eldric moved to the edge of the partition that shielded him—every muscle tense as he looked around.

"How nice of you to join us."

The archcleric's voice rang out, and Eldric's eyes widened as he saw them standing, Lorali bound on the ground before them. Sage's cunning smile cut like a slash across their face.

"I believe that we have business to attend to."

"Let her go," Eldric's voice rasped. He stood motionless, not looking away from Sage's unnervingly smooth gait, like a snake waiting to strike.

"You are as predictable as you are dull."

The archcleric tsked with a shake of their head, their voice dripping with disdain as they stepped around her like she was nothing more than a statue.

"Too loyal to leave, instead following your bond straight to me. I suppose I should thank you, though. Now we can complete our deal." They smiled, motioning towards the center of the room beneath the skylight where Eldric and Lorali had first been bound.

Eldric swallowed, feeling his heart race as he desperately searched for a way to save them both. He couldn't see a way out. It was a harsh reality that he had to face—he was powerless against the might of the archcleric.

"She'll be safe," Eldric reaffirmed with a whisper, muscles wound tight as he dared to glance at Lorali with her wide eyes and motionless frame. "Swear it. Swear on Ostara's name that she'll be safe."

The archcleric's brows pinched together as they stopped before him, voice soft as if they didn't want Lorali to overhear. "I swear on Ostara's name that everything will be as it was. She will be safe, free to make her own choices. Allowing the gallows bond was a mistake, but I will spare her the pain of losing you. It will be as if Eldric Lorecaster never existed. Her life will go back to what it was before you—perfect."

Eldric's blood turned to ice, his breath leaving him. It was this—having the stain of his existence scrubbed from her mind—or death for them both. There was no choice.

"Okay."

CHAPTER 34

LORALI

THE WAY ELDRIC PALED made her mind go silent. There was no escape for them now that he was here. The flicker of his eyes toward her made Lorali's heart squeeze, and she wanted to run to him. But she was trapped, caught in the binds of Sage's magic. They bid her to stand as they neared and that restraining light pulled her upright, placing her feet firmly on the ground. She lifted her chin in defiance.

"Get it over with." Her throat burned as she forced the words out through gritted teeth. She would not die voiceless. She would not go quietly.

The archcleric turned to her, a sympathetic smile upon their face.

"Soon, Lorali," they promised, fingers brushing strands of loose hair away from her face. "All will be as it should be."

The archcleric's magic guided her steps beneath the sky-light filled with twilight stars, that precious time where the moon and sun were in harmony.

"I'm sorry," she said as she stood before Eldric, each word a scorching coal in her throat. The ones she could not speak sat like a weight in her chest.

I'm sorry I ran and didn't stop to listen. I'm sorry I didn't trust you.

She wanted nothing more than to reach out, to touch him. Memorize the feel of him beneath her palm and know the depths of his soul. Lorali struggled against Sage's magic, but it was no use. So she did the only thing she could: she drank in the sight of him. If these were to be their last moments together, she would memorize him. No matter his unkempt hair or weeks of thick stubble that lined his jaw. Hold him in her heart until the bitter end.

"You have nothing to be sorry for, Lor." Eldric's hands came to the sides of her face, sinking into her hair and pulling her forehead to his lips, whispering against her skin. "It'll be okay. I promise."

"Not afraid," she whispered, looking up at him. The words came easier this time, the magic's grip loosening as the archcleric's concentration was pulled by something else. "To die at your side."

The knot in his throat bobbed, eyes shining with unshed tears.

"You will not die today."

There was an unmistakable sadness in his words, as if their fates were no longer intertwined. Her eyes were drawn to the flowing white robes of Sage, who meticulously poured a thick circle of salt around them, creating a protective barrier.

"What are—" Eldric's hands caught her cheeks before she could turn away.

"Don't—just—just let me look at you. One last time," he was pleading, and she couldn't help but shake her head.

"What did you do?" she whispered, desperate as she looked into his eyes, bright as the summer clovers in Juelton.

"There is a way to break the bond. To save you. You'll be okay. I promise." His voice cracked, thick and rough with tears that fell over his winter-paled cheeks.

"No—" Her lips parted, the strangled sound of her voice catching as the archcleric turned their attention back on her. She wanted to scream, to beg.

No, he could not leave her. Not when they had finally found each other. When she finally understood what it meant to live.

"It's time." Sage's voice carried throughout the empty temple hall. She could see the archcleric standing at the edge of the circle from the corner of her eye, waiting with a pitying look upon their face. "It is for the best, Lorali."

Her eyes snapped back to Eldric—her bonded, her friend—as his hand slid from her cheek, down her waist, and unsheathed the dagger at her side. With a tender touch, he lifted her fair-freckled palm skyward, the same way it had been on the grey day they met. He pressed the blade into her skin, and let ruby blood spill across the dark spiraling ink of their bond.

She reveled in the blessed pain they shared as his calloused palm squeezed her own. As their blood mingled for the last time, a final reminder that they lived, their fates sealed by the archcleric's invocation of Athanasios plunging them into a never-ending abyss.

***

Lorali braced herself for the biting cold of Athanasios' realm, the feeling of ice-flooded veins that seeped down into her very soul—but it never came. She felt the weight of Sage's magic on her physical body, but here she felt the call and pull of her own magic once more. Eyes blinking open, she peered into what should have been a starless void to find a twinkling twilight. Her brows furrowed as she looked about the aether realm. There was no god, no dark throne. Only she and Eldric stood on a mirror-like surface that rippled beneath their feet with hands intertwined in a realm equally balanced on the blade of night and day.

Lorali's mind raced, attempting to make sense of the realm of deep purples and blues mixed with fading yellows and burning reds that clashed like the edges of sunset. Sage did not make mistakes—if they meant to send them to Athanasios, it would be done. But neither the dark night of Athanasios, nor the bright sun of Ostara, greeted them. Instead, they were somewhere in between. Light and dark in equal parts. Balanced, as they were each equinox. With a gasp, she realized they stood in the seamlessly blended realms of the god and goddess.

Eldric, she whispered, soul to soul, squeezing his hand tight. His eyes, lined with silver tears, fluttered open at last. She watched as he took in their surroundings as she had, searching for the dark god, to no avail.

Where is he? Eldric's grip tightened on her hand.

I don't know, Lorali admitted as she looked at him with unwavering determination. *But we are not breaking the bond.*

Don't make me fail you again. Let me set things right. His voice was pleading. She felt his anguish, his grief. How much he loathed himself for things beyond his control.

You aren't sacrificing yourself. Whatever happens, we will face it together, she promised, placing a hand over his heart.

There is no way out, Lorali. Her name was a plea on his lips. *This is it. Let me save you.*

You don't get to break our bond on your own. I came here to free you, and I will. We'll get out of this—find somewhere that no one knows us. Take new names, start new lives. Together. Lorali's heart raced as she uttered it, sounding more confident than she felt. With everything reduced to ash, she needed to pause and reassess her plans, to rethink their next steps. As long as they were here, together, there was time. She cradled his face, brushing away his tears. The touch of her hand caused his eyes to fill with a bittersweet blend of hope and desperation that melted her heart. His voice was low as he covered her hand with his own, nodding in agreement. Sealing their promise with one word.

Together.

With the realm slipping into night, they joined forces, their minds racing with ideas on how to flee from their captor. To take back the circlet the archcleric had stolen and make it out in one piece. Despite the impossible odds, they stood together with hope coursing through their veins and tried to prepare as the darkening realm seemed to flicker around them.

With the disappearance of the last ray of sunlight beneath the mirrored horizon, a rush of cool night air filled the space. They both felt the overwhelming, suffocating presence making it hard to breathe—and they knew. The dark void, like a tangible force, curled at Athanasios' heels as he stalked towards them. Gone was the gentle god who dried her tears—in his place stood fury given form. Eldric's grip on her tightened.

Lord Athanasios, she began as he neared, stepping in front of Eldric as if she could somehow protect him from the oncoming storm. Without words, the god flicked his wrist and Lorali felt Eldric's form vanish beneath her fingertips. Her eyes widened as she looked back to where he'd stood with her to find herself alone, and the bond inked within her skin burned away with searing pain. She couldn't catch her breath or even blink, as a scream lodged itself in her throat.

Gone.

He was gone, just like that.

In an instant, her entire world vanished as if it had never existed. Within a heartbeat, the god of the void materialized before her, his eyes fixed on the lone star twinkling in his desolate realm. Her every instinct screamed at her to run as his night-cold voice seeped into her veins like frost on a winter night.

It was with sudden, crashing clarity that she realized the god had only called her by the epithet bestowed during their first encounter, never uttering her name.

Until now.

CHAPTER 35

ELDRIC

SOUND AND NOISE BLURRED together, the hair on his arms prickling as the bleary world swam into focus. He blinked, then blinked again, his eyes adjusting to the soft glow of the full moonlight illuminating the temple's skylight. One moment he was in the divine realm, the next he was here. He shouldn't be alive, not unless they were both back. Eldric lifted his hand and the sight of bare skin instead of the trailing dark ink of their bond struck fear into his heart.

No.

He couldn't make out the shouted words around him through his ringing ears. He turned onto his side, gasping for breath, and reached out with his empty hand, desperately searching for her. The air was filled with the familiar metallic scent of magic that made his limbs quiver with power. As if lightning were about to strike. But it didn't matter as his fingers tightened around hers. His blurred world sharpened as he squeezed it again. Her hand was there, beside him, still and cold. Lifeless.

No.

The word echoed throughout him as he forced his eyes to focus on their entwined fingers. Eldric crawled on his forearms, feeling the strain in every muscle as he pulled himself towards her. Every movement was torture. He didn't care, pushing past the burning pain until he was at her side. Ignoring the shouts and magic that filled the room as he gazed down at her frost-kissed skin. He couldn't find even a thready beat of her heart, and he felt his shatter.

Her once radiant freckles, which dusted her cheeks like constellations, now appeared dull, as if she were still trapped within Athanasios' realm. A chill entered the air and he couldn't tear his eyes away as frozen fractals crept across the ground, radiating from beneath Lorali's body. Tendrils of dark ice crawled outward, stopping at the edges of the salt circle. Emitting an iridescent, otherworldly glow that shimmered in the moonlight.

A roaring wind swept through the room—a magic he was all too familiar with—and he glanced back to see Daeson, lost prince of Athera, with magic pounding through his veins. The archcleric, so focused on their opponent, couldn't spare even a glance toward the cleric and the convict with burning cold seeping into his bones. Their shouts were garbled, as if he were underwater and swimming toward the surface.

"No," he whispered, the small puffs of his breath visible. His hands trembled as he gently caressed her cheeks, as if his touch would bring her back. Her arm was bare of their gallows bond, upturned palm smeared with their blood. With a surge of magic, Eldric cursed under his breath as the building shook around them, protesting in the face of power. Pebbles rained down, air growing heavy with the scent of dust and ancient stone that mingled with the sharp tang of magic. His arms caging her, he dropped to shield her body with his own. Unwilling to leave her, hands tightening in her hair. Eyes closed, praying it wasn't true. Praying that she would come back to him.

When the rumbling finally ceased, he cautiously opened his eyes, his heart skipping a beat as he saw her eyes wide open, locked onto his own. Unseeing. Desolate as the void. The overwhelming presence of a god that made his stomach drop and his breath catch.

Move. The voice was simultaneously Lorali's, but not. Mixed with the masculine undertone of Athanasios. Eldric stumbled to his feet as Lorali, or rather the god channeling himself through her, sat up and slowly eyed the salt circle surrounding them with displeasure. He stepped backwards, outside of the circle, careful not to disrupt it.

"Promise you'll give her back," he whispered to the god, their eyes locked.

Lorali's raised eyebrow and smug smirk were unsettling, so unlike her, it sent shivers down his spine. *I would not separate you. She could not bear it.*

As Eldric looked down at the salt circle, his heart raced, pounding loudly in his ears. Could he trust that the old god would release her, bring her back from the depths of his realm in one piece? Between shaky breaths, he looked back to the chaos unleashing itself behind him. Daeson and Sage were evenly matched. Would they ever stop unless someone forced them? He didn't know what could, outside of divine intervention. So, taking a deep breath, Eldric slid his foot forward and disrupted the grains, breaking the circle and releasing Athanasios into the world.

The chill in the air intensified, wrapping around him like a spectral embrace as that dark ice burst into the rest of the temple hall, transforming it into a frozen realm. It was over before Eldric could even blink as the two sorcerers stilled in an instant.

Much better, the deity remarked with a lilt so reminiscent of Lorali's that it almost fooled him, except for the subtle dissonance. Eldric watched as she descended the stairs with light steps into the surrounding disaster, following at a cautious distance. Wooden planks from shattered pews were strewn across the stone floor. The large stained glass windows completely destroyed. Paintings, vases, statues, art—all of it had fallen and crumbled during the fray.

What the archcleric has done in the name of my beloved has been a source of grief for her all these years, the god murmured, circling a finger in the air as a dark tendril wove itself around Sage's body, restraining them with a frown. *I wish she had let me interfere, but she had hope that things would change. How unfortunate that they didn't.*

With a curious expression on his face, Athanasios stopped in front of the archcleric's frozen form and tilted his head from side to side, as if he were trying to figure something out.

She won't let me end them, the god murmured, fascinated and perplexed. When the silence continued, Eldric cleared his throat, voice catching on itself.

"Ostara?"

No, her little star. The god was quiet, thoughtful for a moment. As if he were listening to something no one else could hear.

*I would grant her any request as a token of gratitude for allowing me to inhabit her mortal vessel despite the dangers. Revenge, power, ascension to the divine. And yet...*Athanasios smiled with a hum. *All she asks for is to return. To you.*

Eldric's breath whooshed out of him. Lorali was in there—alive. And she wanted to come home. He nodded his head over and over as a stupid grin spread across his face, his chest filling with hope.

"Good. She made a few promises to me that she needs to keep."

Athanasios chuckled, shaking his head. Breaking the spell that paralyzed Daeson with a snap, the god watched him crumple to the ground. The fae prince gasped for breath, his chest rising and falling rapidly as he looked around with wide eyes.

Complete your conveyance, child of Sylvene, the god said with mild annoyance. *The former archcleric is yours to do with as you please. A gift from my vessel.*

Daeson looked to the altar where the circlet of Sylvene waited. Sensing the shift in Lorali's power, Daeson asked no questions as he swiftly moved towards the diadem.

Then the god turned to Eldric, giving him a knowing smile. *Take care of her.*

Eldric nodded as Lorali's vacant stare transformed. She blinked, disoriented as the light returned to her eyes and chased away the darkness that had consumed her. He caught her as her knees gave out, guiding them to the ground. He held her there and watched her light hair darken, as if forever changed by the god that had inhabited her. Eldric watched the rise and fall of her even breaths, felt the beating of her heart beneath his palm; she was okay. She was safe.

He shielded his eyes from a sudden, piercing light as he turned and saw the silver and moonstone circlet glow beneath Daeson's touch; a bright and radiant light enveloping him as he lifted it. The crown fit as if it were made for him, shining bright against his dark hair.

A surge of energy coursed through the temple, air crackling with anticipation as everything fell into place. The land's magic righting itself once more as its rightful heir took the crown.

CHAPTER 36

LORALI

A KNOCK ON THE door made Lorali jump and her magic, rich with Athanasios' residual power, burst forth. She cursed, dropping the sixth pitcher she'd frozen this week. As dark ice spread beneath her feet, Lorali stepped away warily. Forcing herself to concentrate on counting her controlled breaths until it not only disappeared, but melted into the cool stone.

She was like a child again, magic eluding her control when she least expected it. Having a divine being inhabit one's body without proper precautions or preparations was bound to have repercussions; her body and magic felt as if they had been stretched beyond their limits. She had not left the temple in the two weeks since Veridian—half of which she had been unconscious, half of which she spent relearning what it meant to control her magic with little progress.

With a final, weary breath, Lorali called out, "Come in."

"Another one?" Heinrich asked as he peeked his head around the door with a wince.

"After I shattered the third, I've only been given steel containers," she joked, picking the container off the floor and setting it on her nightstand. "What can I help you with, Hein?"

"Our new king wishes you to join him for lunch," he said in that playful, singsong voice of his as a grin spread across his face.

"Do you know what for?"

"Nary a clue, but if it means I get to see him? I'm coming with."

"You don't need an excuse. You are literally his emissary and advisor. It's your job to see him." A gentle chuckle escaped Lorali's lips as she draped a cloak over her shoulders, feeling the softness of the fabric against her skin. She glanced at her reflection in the window, her hair slightly messy as she pulled it out from beneath the cloak. She still couldn't get used to the sight of her once starlight hair now darkened by Athanasios' touch.

Everything was changing, and she didn't know if things would ever go back to the way they were. Nothing in Athera would. Or, perhaps, it had returned to its normal that had been long forgotten.

"All thanks to you," he said with a soft grin, leaning against the doorframe as he waited for her.

"Anytime. I think your new job may be worse than being archcleric," she joked, her voice cheerful as she tried to hide the weariness she felt as she walked past him. "C'mon, let's get this over with."

She couldn't help the tangle of nerves and dread bubbling in her stomach as Heinrich shut the door behind them and fell into step beside her. He knew why she was being summoned, but couldn't tell her—his usually bright smile didn't reach his eyes, and that made her worry.

Whatever it was, it must not be anything good.

***

The atrium was filled with daylight. Tables and chairs were pushed towards the edges, covered in Daeson's calculated plans for how to transition Athera into his control. Lorali had missed most of the process during her recovery, something she was grateful for. It felt as if she had fallen asleep in one world and awakened in another, where the streets were settled and the tension had eased. Sage had been tried and executed before the new Atheran court. With Sylvene's circlet gracing his brow, it seemed as if everything had gone according to Daeson's will. Though if Heinrich were to be believed, negotiations with the city council were tumultuous at best. Trying to work with the existing government rather than overthrowing them. He had convinced the newly- anointed king that in order to rule, it was not just the crown upon his head he needed, but the heart of the people as well.

Lorali's senses sharpened as she picked up on the angry hushed whispers growing louder with each step they took down the hall. After she turned into the atrium, her attention was drawn to Eldric's stormy expression, his finger forcefully pressed against Daeson's chest.

"This is not a compromise," he hissed, loud enough to echo off the high glass ceiling. Heinrich cleared his throat and the two looked up, Eldric's gaze furious as it first landed on Heinrich then softening as it found her.

"High Cleric Wynmar, Emissary Holst—thank you for coming." Daeson stepped away to greet them as if everything were normal. Eldric stalked past his friend, moving to Lorali's side with a firm jaw. The intensity of his anger was almost tangible as he glared at Daeson, making the air around them feel suffocating.

"Am I expected to use formalities now?" Lorali asked, trying to keep her voice light. Daeson's chuckle was empty as he shook his head.

"No. Come, let us eat and then—"

"I'd prefer it if we cut to the chase." Lorali countered, lips pressed together into a tight smile as she looked at the new king of Athera. "Tell me the reason you've called me here. You know I'm not one for politics and pleasantries."

Eldric snorted, and she nudged her elbow into his side.

"So I've learned," Daeson agreed, taking a deep breath before continuing. "The city council expects you and Eldric to atone for failing to complete the terms of your gallows bond. Eldric was arrested and though your bond is... *annulled,* they say it is the only way they will move forward with negotiations. They want to move forward with your original punishment, but I've convinced them you would best serve Athera alive. Both of you." The king's voice was tight as he looked down at her, hands clasped behind his back. Eldric's silence put her on edge and Lorali's brow furrowed as she read between the lines.

"Will we be free to leave?"

Daeson closed his eyes, pressing his lips into a thin line. "Your work would be compulsory. You'd be bound in Athera's service."

This is not a compromise, Eldric had said. Staying in the city they called home meant choosing between this or death.

She understood. Faced with uncertainty, there was no choice but to prioritize the needs of the city over his personal attachments. If this meant getting the city council's cooperation and a peaceful transition into his rule, then she knew she couldn't hold it against him.

Yet, the thought of staying in her tiny house perched on the hillside—with its lush garden and wild ivy crawling across the stone—until her skin wrinkled and hair greyed, wasn't the comfort it once had been. She wanted more than the forest cottage with its small garden and empty rooms she had once called home. Yearned to conquer the towering Vikal mountains and uncover the hidden enchantments they held within. See ocean waves crashing onto the sandy beach of her hometown, while the piercing calls of gulls soaring overhead filled the air. Wanted a life outside of Athera, to go wherever her feet may fall with someone at her side. Perhaps home wasn't where you ran to, but who you ran with.

Pulling the keys from her waistbelt, Lorali unclasped and pressed the steel into Heinrich's palm with a resolute nod. "The cottage is yours. Don't kill my plants."

Her brother's knowing smile was wide and bright as he pulled her into a hug.

"I wouldn't dream of it," he whispered into her hair, gripping her tighter.

"Lorali, what are you doing?" Daeson's tanned skin paled as he asked a question he already seemed to know the answer to.

"I think I've served this city long enough," she said, words hanging in the air as she extended her hand towards Eldric.

"Run away with me." It wasn't a question, but an offering. To follow where the other may lead—dive into the unknown and discover who they were. To have faith.

As the rogue's lazy smile stretched across his face, her heart pounded in her chest. With a mischievous glint in his eyes, he quirked his eyebrow as he looked down at her. "Do I even have a choice?"

She grinned and her eyes, for the first time in a long time, were alight with the promise of tomorrow. "It's this or death. I assume you prefer the former."

"Well, when you put it that way, how could I possibly refuse?" Tucking a loose strand of hair behind her ear, Eldric's smile melted into a gentle expression.

"El, don't do this." Daeson's eyes were wide, and he whispered, almost pleaded, as he gripped his friend's sh oulder."You'll be branded a criminal. I'll have to place a bounty on your head. You can never return. Just take the offer."

"All of that only matters if I'm caught," Eldric said, as his arms enveloped Daeson in a tight embrace. Conveying more than words ever could.

"Thank you for everything," Daeson murmured as he clung to him, his deep breath dissolving into a chuckle. "Just know that if your ass gets caught, I might not be able to save you."

"I happen to be pretty good at evading the law; been kind of doing it for quite a while now." Eldric laughed as they parted.

"You were caught. Twice. Your track record is less than stellar." Daeson teased Eldric with a mischievous look.

"He's got a point," Heinrich agreed as Lorali said, "Good thing we're owed a complimentary head start."

Eldric gaped, placing a hand over his heart. "Maybe it's a good thing we're leaving. I don't think I could survive dealing with all three of you at once."

Bittersweet laughter echoed throughout the atrium.

"I think it's time for us to run," Lorali said, slipping her hand into Eldric's with a soft smile. Her eyes glistened with unshed tears, despite knowing this goodbye wasn't forever. But as their footsteps echoed off the temple's ancient stone walls, clicked across cobbled stone, and raced down the dirt-trodden path that led them home, she couldn't help as they fell.

Excitement couldn't outweigh the grief as she left a piece of herself behind. Lorali had buried it in the garden soil with him, watered it with her tears. With each passing day since they had met, it grew stronger and more vibrant until it was time for the seeds to scatter on the wind as they prepared to leave Athera far, far behind.

And, hand in hand, they did.

Epilogue

POWERFUL GUSTS OF WIND battered the coastal city, pushing sails across the vast expanse of the sea and toward the port. Lorali pulled strands of short, dark hair from her mouth and tucked them behind her ear as she enjoyed the sun warming her skin after months spent in the cold, magic-filled mountains in Isodore.

"Where do you want to go?" Eldric asked, sun-bronzed arms folded behind his head as he closed his eyes and listened to the sound of crashing waves. With a small smile playing on her lips, she watched him. Finding joy in the way he basked in the sunlight and reminded her of a contented dog reveling in its favorite sunspot.

"I'm not sure. I didn't really think this far ahead," she answered truthfully. "Any ideas?"

Eldric rolled onto his side, head propped into his hand as he looked at her with a grin. "This is one of the biggest port cities in the world, so wherever we want, we can go."

Lorali's brows furrowed, frowning at the old map held down in the sand by shells and faded with age with careful consideration. Her finger followed the ley lines she had added to their map, settling on a large lake surrounded by mountains farther up the Korinth coast. "I think this may be the place. Someone at the hostel said there's an impressive library that holds any text or scroll you could imagine," she said with a definitive nod.

"Your obsession with magical history never ceases to amaze me. Turning our second marriage ceremony into another research trip," Eldric chuckled with a shake of his head as he flopped back into the sand.

She raised her brow after a moment, a smile creeping across her face, her necklace holding her parents' wedding bands slipping from beneath her shirt and dangling in the space between them as she leaned over him. "What was that?"

He grinned, loving their little game as he looked up into her clear eyes that sparkled with a joy he had grown to love seeing in them. His knuckles grazed across her freckled skin.

"Nothing," he hummed, his eyes lighting up with anticipation as she leaned in. "Just that I can't wait for you to be my wife again."

Their noses touched as her breath caressed his skin, their lips brushing against each other as she spoke.

"That's what I thought."

THE END

Acknowledgements

First things first, I would like to acknowledge myself. You did it, bitch. You wrote the damn book. I am so proud of you. Happy Birthday.

Now, for the rest. Because writing a book is like raising a baby—it takes a village. And without my village, I wouldn't be here right now. Consider this dedication round two.

To Courtney Dold, my dearest friend and fiercest champion—thank you for your unwavering, full hearted belief in everything I do. I will forever be grateful that you worked up the courage to message me first when we were both staring at each other's profiles on tiktok, too scared to press send. None of this could have ever happened without you. I would have set down my pen long ago. Every semicolon, I dedicate to you. Thank you, love you, see you soon.

To Kathrine Sweet, my confidant. You have listened and held space for me more times than I can count. When I've needed it most and the chips were down, you have always been there to lend a hand and lift me up once more. It is a wonderful thing to find someone you can message at all hours and know without a doubt you aren't a bother. Someone to send your novel to chapter by chapter. To sit in the silence with and know it's okay. We joke that we're actually the same virgo separated by 20 years, but if I grow up to be half the woman you are, I'll have done something good with myself.

To Kelsey Snook, my comma Queen. Thank you for your immeasurable patience and willingness to work with me when my time blindness kicked in. You saved my manuscript one painstaking comma at a time and made the editing process of my first novel a breeze, especially after things went upside down with my original editor. I'm so glad we found each other and I can't wait to work with you on many manuscripts to come.

To my badass betas—you are literal rockstars. Every sentence you touched has made this novel better. Linnea, you're the first person IRL I told about my secret online life as an author outside of my husband. Thank you for being my rock throughout college, into adulthood, and for the many years ahead. Leo, the stars aligned in a super weird way for us to connect. And then reconnect all these years later. You had such an impact on my writing journey when I was a young college freshman trying to find herself. Thank you for being weird with me on the internet. Stay groovy. Jada, you're an inspiration. I'm honestly honored and awed that we're not only part of each others developmental teams, but friends. You remind me to keep aiming higher.

To my family—Mom, thank you for always believing in my writing and teaching me to stand tall. Dad, thank you for showing me what it means to own your life and forge your own path. Jeremy and Drew, please know that publishing a book officially makes me The Coolest Sibling ™ out of the three of us. I already had that title, but this cemented it.

To my cat, Ghost, who never understood why I had to lock her out the room because she only wanted to sit on my keyboard. I love you and promise to buy you a new cat tree when I break even on this book.

To my husband, Konrad. You've seen it all, I've said it all. There's plenty more to say, but it's nothing that you don't already know. Love you v much. & Thank you for having an awesome last name.

To my fellow authors and writers of all kinds—but especially my friends at the Second Cup Writer's Cafe—*keep writing*. Write every word with reckless abandon. Your words are needed. They will change the world.

And to you, my dearest reader. If you have picked up my book and given it a chance, thank you from the very depths of my soul. I hope you find yourself in these words. That you come away just a little more healed than when you found them.

ABOUT THE AUTHOR

Elizabeth Skarpnes is a life-long writer who is finally putting words to the page. Her works explore themes of trust, experiencing new cultures, and leaving home for the first time through the lens of powerful female characters.

She is a writer by necessity, developmental editor by passion, and nurse by trade. She owns the Second Cup Writers Cafe, a community for writers to connect with others and make friends.

Join her newsletter at www.elizabethskarpnes.com for an exclusive bonus scene of Eldric & Lorali's future!

FALL ^{OF} ^{THE} DRAGON KING

COMING SOON

Reading Guide

Scan the QR code to be taken to the Reader Guide for more To The Gallows content including an annotated playlist, character profiles, and more! Search for the hidden portal there to learn more the secret history of the world of To The Gallows.

www.ingramcontent.com/pod-product-compliance
Lightning Source LLC
Chambersburg PA
CBHW022020310726
48972CB00006B/1738